The
SINGING
GURU

❋

‹ *Book One of the Sikh Saga* ›

The
SINGING
GURU

❊

LEGENDS AND ADVENTURES OF
GURU NANAK, THE FIRST SIKH

Kamla K. Kapur

Foreword by
Nikky-Guninder Kaur Singh

MANDALA
PUBLISHING

San Rafael, California

MANDALA
PUBLISHING

PO Box 3088
San Rafael, CA 94912
www.mandalaeartheditions.com

Find us on Facebook: www.facebook.com/mandalaearth
Follow us on Twitter: @mandalaearth

Library of Congress Cataloging-in-Publication Data available.
ISBN: 978-1-60887-503-0

INSIGHT EDITIONS
Publisher: Raoul Goff
Co-publisher: Michael Madden
Art Director: Chrissy Kwasnik
Designer: Jenelle Wagner
Executive Editor: Vanessa Lopez
Project Editor: Courtney Andersson
Production Editor: Rachel Anderson
Production Manager: Jane Chinn

ROOTS of PEACE REPLANTED PAPER
Insight Editions, in association with Roots of Peace, will plant two
trees for each tree used in the manufacturing of this book. Roots of
Peace is an internationally renowned humanitarian organization dedicat-
ed to eradicating land mines worldwide and converting war-torn lands
into productive farms and wildlife habitats. Roots of Peace will plant
two million fruit and nut trees in Afghanistan and provide farmers there
with the skills and support necessary for sustainable land use.

Manufactured in China by Insight Editions

10 9 8 7 6 5 4 3 2 1

For my father,
Brigadier Hardit Singh Kapur,
Who always wanted me to write this book;
And my mother, Lajwant Kaur,
A sixteenth-generation descendant of Guru Nanak,
Who has told me these stories,
Dramatizing them in repeated retellings.

ੴ

Contents

Preface IX

Foreword.. XVII

PART I: WANDERING

1. Mardana, the Unhappy Human 3

2. Rabab.. 13

3. Mardana Finds a Treasure 27

4. Throw Away the Bundle 41

5. A Good Bargain 47

6. What the River Said 59

7. An Encounter with Thugs 67

8. At the Friend's House 75

9. Stone 85

10. Gem 95

11. From the Roof of the Fish's Belly 109

12. Rondoo's Sacrifice 119

13. The Red Mark 125

14. The Glowing Eyes of Death 131

15. The Fortress 137

16. Grinding Wheels 143

17. Lord of Desire 153

18. City of God 161

19. Homecoming 171

PART II: SEEDS

20. Shehzada 179

21. In His Orchard 185

22. At the Dera 191

23. Ashes and Gold 201

24. Epilogue, Prologue 207

Bibliography 209

Acknowledgments 215

Preface

I grew up with Guru Nanak. I was a child when my father told me the story that every Sikh child knows: Guru Nanak, in his many travels, went from India to Mecca, the Muslim holy city. Tired after his long and arduous journey, he fell asleep with his feet pointing toward the *Ka'aba*.[1] The *mullah*[2] of the mosque shook him rudely and said, "Infidel! How dare you sleep with your dirty feet pointing toward God?"

The angry *mullah* picked up Guru Nanak's feet and swung them around in the opposite direction—but then the *Ka'aba* swung around too. Whichever direction the astounded *mullah* turned Guru Nanak's feet, the *Ka'aba* was there, facing his feet.

My father explained to me that the point of the story is that God is everywhere, in every direction, in every space, without exception. This concept confused me, and I found myself wondering how God could be in the tank full of sewage in our neighborhood. That night I had a dream—the first that I recall—in which Guru Nanak, his long white beard rippling like a river of silk, arose from the scum of the sewage tank wearing a perfectly clean long white robe, took me in his arms, and cuddled up next to me in bed.

Ever since that dream, Guru Nanak has been my Second Guide. He slept with me when I was frightened, and he took me on the ultimate journey, the

---

[1] A cuboid building at the center of Islam's most sacred mosque in Mecca, Saudi Arabia.
[2] A Muslim cleric educated in Islamic theology and sacred law.

one that makes all literal journeys pale shadows of the Real Thing; the journey Nanak calls "the pilgrimage to ourselves."

It is a relationship that has had conflicts, quarrels, separations, sudden closeness, and long distances. During my period of rebellion, which lasted some twenty-five years, Guru Nanak seemed absent until suddenly, like an underground root that spreads and sprouts in another continent, he reappeared in 1989 while I was in the United States. It was four and a half years before a personal tragedy struck.

It is a constant source of amazement to me that while on this Real Journey, our soul prepares for the direction the journey will take long before our conscious mind becomes aware of it.

I recall the exact instance when Guru Nanak sprang alive in my consciousness again, just as if he had never been away those many years. It was shortly after my marriage to Donald Dean Powell. I was walking on the beach listening to some *kirtan*[3] tapes I had picked up on a whim during a visit to India. At the first few holy sounds, my parched soul ignited into an unquenchable fire. The divine had entered through the portals of my ears.

Though I grew up listening to kirtan on the radio and on phonograph records—both my parents were ardent fans—this felt entirely new. It riveted my heart, mind, and soul. My future direction was pouring its melody into my years. Henceforth, I bought and listened to *shabads*[4] incessantly. It is a happy addiction to which I owe my life.

At about the same time, a prayer I had heard in my youth began repeating itself in my head: "Taira phaana meetha lagai," meaning "May your will be sweet." Not "May thy will be done," not "May I accept or resign myself to your will," but "May your will be *sweet*." My own interpretation of God's will is the Cosmic will of the Unimultiverse—that which is and cannot be circumvented or reversed.

I didn't know then what I can see so clearly in retrospect: these seemingly sudden occurrences had been ripening all through my rebellious years. This spiritual growth was necessary preparation for death, for the end that we fear for ourselves and those we love, and which we need to remember in order to live consciously, with a passionate and ever-renewed attention to the inevitable passage of time and a commitment to life in all its aspects.

---

[3] Sung text from the Sikh holy book, the Sri Guru Granth Sahib (SGGS).
[4] Divine utterances, holy sounds.

In 1993, my then husband, Donald, committed suicide. When I called my father in India to tell him, his words to me after his initial shock and sorrow were "Take it lightly," and "It is part of the design." My father is (and continues to be, even after his death in 2007) my Third Guide, the one who brought me to the other two.

The story of how my husband's death taught me to live better, to love again, and to find sweetness in sadness, is a long one, perhaps never to be told in full, though a part of it was told in my book-length poem, *As a Fountain in a Garden.*

Kirtan, music accompanied by the songs of the gurus, gave me a place to turn to when all my ways were lost. The music provided me with a space to inhabit where all is forever well, where nothing is lost. It gave the rivers of my tears an ocean to pour into. It gave meaning to my suffering and illumined my darkness.

Though I grieved long and hard, it seemed my hand was held through this crisis, a hand that has never withdrawn itself since. Throughout these years, a strong chord has tied me to Guru Nanak, my Second Guide, whose words echoing in my ears have helped me steer through the turbulent waters of life. Guru Nanak unceasingly points his finger to the invisible and ever-present First Guide, the Adi,[5] the primeval Purush,[6] the One beyond dualities and the clashing swords of conflict; the Formless suffused through form, the Invisible manifest in the visible, the Mother-Father Energy of the universe, neither male nor female; a nondifferentiated Being, beyond human conception and Naming (yet responsive to the names we attribute to It), and as near to us as our heart, blood, and skin; the One who is the Axis on which the universe turns, the protoplasm that flows through every sentient creature, through every miniscule and petty detail of our lives and all the levels of who we are. Guru Nanak's words, echoing in my ears, have been my holy guides.

I am eclectic about spiritual wisdom, and glean it from all sources. I have written two books from the Hindu and Muslim traditions: *Ganesha Goes to Lunch* (U.S.; now reprinted in India as *Classics from Mystic India*) and *Rumi's Tales from the Silk Road* (U.S.; published in India as *Pilgrimage to Paradise: Sufi Tales*

---

[5] Primordial.

[6] From Sanskrit, the Cosmic Principle, Consciousness, the Self, personified for man's emotional needs as the Cosmic Man.

from Rumi). This eclecticism and egalitarianism is an integral part of Sikhism. The Sri Guru Granth Sahib (SGGS), the Sikh holy book, contains the songs (called *bani*[7]) of seven Sikh gurus, including Guru Nanak, who composed and sang; the songs of fifteen Hindu and Sufi saints, such as Jaidev, Ramanand, Farid, and Kabir; and the songs of six low-caste, "untouchable" saints (cobblers, butchers, barbers), such as Ravidas, Sain, and Sadhana.

Guru Nanak's definition of a religious person is "one who looks on all as equal." Brotherhood and sisterhood of all on this planet is Sikhism's basic tenet; music is at its heart; and the worship of words, *akhar*,[8] *naam*,[9] and shabad is at its very core.

Guru Nanak's (1469–1539) spiritual fire sparked the world's youngest religion, Sikhism, which continued through nine succeeding incarnate gurus and established itself for all time with the compilation of the Eleventh Guru, the Sri Guru Granth Sahib. This holy book is revered as a Living Guru whose spirit is embodied in the Word.

In his youth, Nanak was a wandering poet and minstrel who traveled to the far corners of India and beyond, all the way to the Middle East and China. At a time when a man was distinguished by his garb, Guru Nanak dressed theatrically, combining elements from Islamic and Hindu attire with something of his own, to challenge the preconceived notions of those he met along the way. He sang ecstatically of and to the Beloved Being, the One to whom, Nanak believes, all beings and inanimate creations in the material world sing. Nanak's 974 extant songs, contained in the SGGS, evidence Nanak's vision and experience of the nonsectarian Being, Akal Purakh,[10] the Timeless One beyond gender. It is a vision that illumines the miracle of our presence on this planet and forces a reevaluation of our humdrum, comfortable lives. Nanak's is an inspired marveling that conjures the Other, who is also ourselves, the One subject and object of our highest and most intense longings.

Many other aspects of his multidimensional personality complemented Nanak's mystical nature. He was a social critic, revolutionary, and iconoclast

---

[7]   Sound, music, voice, praise, or laudation. In the Sikh context it means the sacred compositions of the gurus and the holy saints included in the SGGS.

[8]   A word or a character.

[9]   Name.

[10] The Sikh variant of the Vedic Purush. The primeval, creative spirit embodied and personified by the human imagination, but not contained by it.

who reunited mankind with the forces of nature. He said of himself that he had no more caste or race than wind or fire; he blasted through the petty, parochial, limited, superstitious, and encrusted version of God, cut through the delusions and ignorance that separate humans from each other, saw through the skin of appearance to the light that informs every breathing thing, shattered the prescriptions and constrictions of rituals and idolatry, and sought at the source the transcendent and immanent energy infused through the micro- and macrocosm. Nanak's is a personal, direct, and unmediated Way that places no barriers between the lover and the Beloved. In his songs, Nanak rends the perceptual veils that blind us to the truth that the Lord of the cosmos and the human heart are one. This oneness transcends all the stratifications of society.

None of these abstract descriptions can encompass Guru Nanak's totality. He inhabited all of himself. In addition to being a sage and guru, he was also a wanderer, poet, singer, adventurer, son, husband, father, and brother. Later in his life, when he settled down in a city he established—Kartarpur, the City of the Creator—he tilled the fields, sowed seeds, and harvested crops. He used these experiences to weave metaphors of cultivation into many of his songs. In Kartarpur he established the community that became the first followers of the religion we call Sikhism, a community that welcomed people from all walks of life, that ate together in a common kitchen, and worshipped the Essential God, not its fragmented images.

Nanak's message was clear: God had to be found within life through engagement, not withdrawal. A human has to play, and play well, the many roles that life demands. He believed fervently that Karta Purakh, the Creator and Experiencer, was similarly engaged in the drama of existence. Nanak refused nothing of life, but affirmed all of it: the mundane and the spiritual, the practical and philosophic, the human and divine. He was wedded to both God and wife, ecstasy and the quotidian, at once earthbound and ecstatic. For him, the secular and the holy are on the same continuum. Soul and body, God and wife, song and plowing, contemplation and society, meditation and food—he lived a life of full relatedness on every level.

However, Nanak never tires of reminding us that our engagement with all aspects of life has its essential counterpart in detachment; that worldliness and business without personal discipline and a turning to love and adoration of the One will doom a soul to torment.

This book is not a history of Guru Nanak's life. It is a fictional rendering that includes some of the legends, folktales, and myths that have sprung up around him. There are many of them, and I have had to be selective. Nor does this book attempt to follow the chronology of the traditional and canonical version of Guru Nanak's life. Narrative and thematic consistency guided me more than the factual timeline. I followed the practice of chroniclers who wove a context around Guru Nanak's words, though I have parted ways by reinventing the traditionally accepted contexts.

It became clear to me early on in the process of writing that I could not write the book from the point of view of Guru Nanak. In one's smallness it is impossible to encompass, describe, envision, or recreate a being as spacious as he. Instead, I chose to view Nanak through the very human eyes of Mardana, his servant, accompanist on the rabab, disciple, and companion.

While growing up, I listened to stories about Mardana that were interwoven with stories about Guru Nanak. In the Punjabi folk tradition, he is a Sancho Panza–like character at the animal end of the human spectrum. I have retained some of this, though in this book Mardana has evolved into a complex character with a seed of light that luminesces as he gets to the end of his life. Mardana, like the rest of us, is afflicted with vice, haunted by worries, fears, and desires, full of all sorts of hungers, and at the mercy of his untamed mind. He often makes conscious decisions to ignore Nanak's advice. His appetites and many desires always get him into trouble. He is the image of the entrapped soul, bound with a chain and at the mercy of his cravings.

The legends and stories of Guru Nanak's life that I grew up with from the *Janamsakhis*[11] were invariably skeletal. The two fragmentary stories that are the underpinning of this narrative include the time that Mardana became a goat and Guru Nanak rescued him, and the time that Mardana was given a bundle of things that weighed him down in his journeys. Guru Nanak asked him to throw the bundle away, which, according to the traditional version, Mardana obediently did.

These stories are fantastical. Fantasy is part of human reality, not only as an escape hatch from the pressures of the real world, but also because of its power to illuminate reality and reveal metaphysical and psychological truths.

---

[11] The compiled stories and legends of Guru Nanak's life.

Having been a fan of mythology all my life, I sympathize with the popular sentiment that gives wings to facts. Our magical heroes and sacred icons serve as reminders of who we can become.

The story, though complete due to the necessity of an ending, is incomplete in the sense that the narratives of the succeeding nine Sikh gurus carry on through the generations for two more centuries. This is the first of a series of books. Nanak and Mardana will reappear in Book Two, along with their wives and children, who are barely mentioned in this volume. The main thrust of this book has been Guru Nanak and Mardana's odyssey and the adventures and legends associated with it.

Max Arthur Macauliffe, whose labor of love, after much research culled from many sources, produced six prodigious volumes titled *The Sikh Religion: Its Gurus, Sacred Writings and Authors*, and whose work has been the main source and inspiration for this and my subsequent books, starts his volumes with the following words: "I bring from the East what is practically an unknown religion." Though his books were first published in 1909, Sikhism continues to be an unknown and misunderstood religion. Sikhs are often mistaken in the West for Muslim terrorists. It is my humble hope that my work will contribute to an understanding of Sikhism and its founder, whose nondenominational approach to spirituality and joyous acceptance of all aspects of life is particularly relevant in today's fragmented and conflicted world.

Foreword

Those who do not have power over the story that dominates their lives,
the power to retell it, rethink it, deconstruct it, joke about it, and change it as times change,
truly are powerless, because they cannot think new thoughts.
SALMAN RUSHDIE

*T*he Singing Guru is an enchanting retelling of Guru Nanak's life and message in the voice of Bhai Mardana, the Guru's Muslim companion and rabab player. Here Kamla Kapur has chosen a highly innovative and subtle perspective to reveal the historicity and timeless reality of the founding Sikh Guru. Mythic narratives (*sakhis*) about Guru Nanak's birth and life are very popular in the collective Sikh imagination, and have come down in a variety of renditions such as the *Bala*, *Miharban*, *Adi*, and *Puratan*. But when we hear Mardana animatedly talk about a fellow companion he so closely sees and hears, time and space collapse; like Mardana, we begin to feel the numinous magic of the Guru's presence.

Mardana interlaces his meta-narrative of the country ruled by women with many other legends and accounts of his travels with Nanak, whom he endearingly calls "Baba." This ancient story with Nath antecedents has enjoyed immense popularity among the *Janamsakhi* traditions (except for the *Miharban*), and has clearly captured the imagination of our twenty-first-century author. In a way it is a feminist utopia, much like the one dreamed by the Bengali writer Rokeya Hossain (*Sultana's Dream*, 1905), for the women govern all spheres of private and public life, and are highly successful. On the other hand, the legend is misogynist: the women are actually temptresses and sorceresses. In this case, Mardana, having left the guru's company, is lured by the sorceresses and turned into a goat for his captors' meal. It is in the pen—with his fellow goats, all awaiting their death—that Mardana shares Baba's stories. Interestingly, the various protagonists have their own individual character and attitudes represented by their names— Taakat, Mannay, or Rondoo. As Mardana retells, rethinks, and deconstructs the narratives of his beloved Guru, each listens, questions, and responds in different and new ways. The dialogic format reinforces and renews the Guru's teachings in an effective communal setting. And this is the triumph of Kamla Kapur's work: she sets off on a fantastic hermeneutic adventure within a highly charged atmosphere.

We find Baba linked in a dynamic nexus with his family and the larger society. His relationships with his wife and sons, neglected in traditional narratives, are here brought into meaningful discourse. Since Mardana is a fellow villager, he is also able to render a vibrant immediacy to the names and places associated with Guru Nanak. For instance, there is something ineffably warm and personal in his reference to Daulatan (the Muslim midwife who delivered baby Nanak) as "Masi" (mother's sister). Mardana depicts the Guru as an intrinsic part of his vibrant geographical, cultural, and multireligious landscape—a human being like him and his fellow villagers with the same faculties, the same angst, the same tensions, and the same potential. The difference: by living authentically, Baba hones his self and actualizes divinity. In Mardana's words, "I . . . saw how he had made a ladder from the sound of God's name and climbed out of his own darkness. Baba was a man with animal instincts who had become the pinnacle of what a human could be: divine." Thus the divine Guru emerges as a powerful role model. The goats can follow his example and the degenerate, egocentric *manmukhs* can become spiritually oriented *gurmukhs*. In their own and different ways, readers of Kamla Kapur's text will be inspired by the Guru's divine personality and accomplishments, his ethical views, and his metaphysical vision.

The Singing Guru highlights Sikh ethics as a coalescence of the sacred and the secular. This human life is precious, and should not be regarded casually, which

Mardana and his fellow goats had done. All aspects of life are important and must be lived authentically. Family and society must not be rejected. As Mardana reminds us, Baba has no conflict between marriage and God: "He says they are compatible and necessary. God and the world are one; to separate God from life is ignorance and duality." *The Singing Guru* provides the perfect definition of a Sikh as a student who is always eager and passionate to learn how to grow into his or her full potential as a true and conscious human being.

Kamla Kapur's text also expresses the intricacies of Sikh metaphysics in a profoundly simple manner. The Sikh theological reality is the singular One, transcending space, time, gender, and causality, and yet this One permeates each and every finite being. Instead of the mind-body dualism and its harmful hierarchies, the body is exalted with its Divine ingredient. To discover and experience this miraculous element in the daily rhythms is affirmed as the ideal mode of existence—*wah*—full of wonder, amazement, and awe. Kamla Kapur's nuanced explanations advance our comprehension of Guru Nanak's distinct worldview.

The traditional *Janamsakhis* frequently construct concrete scenes to contextualize Nanak's hymns recorded in the Sri Guru Granth Sahib. *The Singing Guru* recreates the symbiosis between his person and word—for after all, the ladder that Baba climbs up is made of sonorous textures of sacred verse. In fact, the way Mardana utilizes the sublime lyrics in the stories he tells and the way in which his audience receives them generate new interpretations, new understandings, and new applications of the Guru's hymns.

Like Mardana's audience, we too may find ourselves at times rolling our eyes and at others craning our neck to hear more. When have we had a chance to slither past a slimy tongue and jostle about in the digestive juices of a fish's belly? Have we ever experienced the daily dawn when "the orb of the full moon glowed like a pearl against the steel blue sky of early morning"? Whether describing the extraordinary or the ordinary, Kamla Kapur delineates her scenes with enormous artistic finesse. This modern writer's use of medieval analogies is particularly compelling. For instance, she uses the Persian wheel, which we frequently hear gurgling in Sikh scripture and see rotating in the visual art of the *Janamsakhis*, to describe Mardana's fluctuating emotions of despair and joy. While deepening our understanding of the past, Kamla Kapur's literary disclosures evoke new possibilities.

At some level, *The Singing Guru* is a replay of Nanak's triple formula, expressed in the Japji: "Sunia mannia mani kita bhau." *Sunia* literally signifies hearing, the sense that most directly connects the conscious and the unconscious realms. Hearing is the first step toward awakening to the transcendent core of the universe, which Mardana is doing by narrating his stories. *Mannia* means remembering the One, and it is the second step, for it is only after something is heard that it can enter the mind. Keeping the Divine constantly in mind is not an entirely intellectual process, because it connotes trust and faith, which are embodied in "Mannay," one of the listeners in the pen. "Mani kita bhau," meaning "full of love for the Divine," is the third step. It goes beyond hearing and keeping the One in mind. Intensely passionate and joyous, love is the death of all fears, phobias, and barriers; it is living out the divine transcendence in the fluctuating fullness of temporality. This love is ignited by the melodious verse coming from the lips of the three-dimensional figure of Baba Nanak resonating off the pages of *The Singing Guru.*

We all owe a deep debt of gratitude to the prolific Kamla Kapur for wonderfully retelling the narrative of the singing guru, who dominates the lives of over twenty-five million people worldwide.

—Nikky-Guninder Kaur Singh
Crawford Family Professor of Religious Studies
Colby College, Waterville, Maine, USA

PART I

Wandering

CHAPTER 1
Mardana, the Unhappy Human

Two pilgrims paused in a bamboo grove to rest on a hot summer afternoon. Nanak, ten years younger than his companion Mardana, hung his wool blanket and few meager belongings on a branch and walked to a tiny spring nearby. He removed fistfuls of dead bamboo leaves and rotting mulch, which had choked its flow, until the clear water overflowed into the adjoining land and fed the thirsty earth.

"Come drink, Mardana," he said to his companion. Sitting at the spring's edge, Nanak cupped his hand and drank.

Mardana took off his satchel, leaned his *rabab*[1]—the musical instrument he was carrying—against a rock, and collapsed on the ground. He felt unable to move, yet severe thirst made him crawl to the spring, put his face to it, and drink like an animal, lapping the water with his tongue. The cool liquid flowing into his parched mouth revived him a little, and he returned to the spot by his rabab and lay down as one dead.

Nanak proceeded to wash and clean himself in the spring before clearing the ground of stones, spreading his blanket, and lying down on it. Soon he was fast asleep.

Mardana lay in a heap, too tired to remove the pebbles or to spread his blanket beneath him. A tired body and an overactive brain kept him too

---

[1] A musical instrument, either plucked or played with a bow, also called *rebec*.

agitated to sleep. He was hungry and uncomfortable, and a vague discontent at having been away from the comforts of home for so long began to brew in Mardana's mind. It quickly turned into a full-blown, raging unhappiness.

How long, how very long have I been away from home? Do I even have a home? Mardana asked himself, repeating the question that had been foremost in his thoughts for quite a while. *Twenty years—maybe more, twenty-two, or three—what am I doing so far away from my homeland, from Fatima, my children, and my dog?*

He looked at Nanak, who he called Baba, resting in the shade of the bamboo grove, his arm folded under his head, his face radiant even in sleep.

Why can't I be like Baba, so certain and centered, so detached from comfort or discomfort, satisfaction and hunger, prosperity and adversity? Mardana thought, stretching upon the ground, longing for something soft beneath his body and head. He felt coarse and altogether too human compared to Nanak. Mardana was aware that he was rather attached to his appetites and vacillated too much between despair and joy. He felt like a Persian waterwheel, sometimes empty like the buckets clanking all the way down, and sometimes full and sloshing with sweet, clear water on the way up. He felt certain of the presence of God when things went his way, when he was provided for—with food when he was hungry, a bed when he was sleepy, and the unexpected boat or bullock cart arriving on the riverbank when his bruised and blistered feet screamed in pain. But in adversity, the thin film of his faith dissolved, and he was certain that this whole philosophic construct of God was nothing but a pipe dream.

The image of the pipe brought with it a whole train of other desires. *I could really do with a bowl full of* bhang[2] *and a jar full of sweet red wine. All these hardships would be worth it if they were followed by some rewards.*

He recalled how once, when Nanak and he had returned home to Sultanpur after a long journey, Fatima had been angry at Mardana and told him to go away and leave her alone. Mardana, upset, had gone to the village bhang shop and had some in a hookah, sitting in a circle with others, all pleasantly high and happy. He had returned home in an amorous mood and made up with Fatima. *Wah! Wah!*[3] Allah[4] himself had descended into their bed and

---

[2] Marijuana.
[3] An expression of wonder, awe, or applause.
[4] Guru Nanak was born a Hindu, and Mardana a Muslim.

bodies that night! As Mardana recalled the scene, his fingers reached out and traced the contours of his wife's absent body.

Doesn't Baba ever miss his wife? Mardana wondered. *He hardly ever speaks about her, or even mentions his two sons. He is wedded to an intangible thing he calls Beloved, Husband, Guru, Akal Purakh, and the Timeless One. But I miss Fatima and the comfort of her in my arms, in our bed, her delicious cooking, and her ministrations when I am sick. Will I ever be with her again? Will I ever reach home and lead an ordinary life?*

Mardana turned his mind to the image of the kind hostess in the last village where Baba and he had rested. Her features and face swam before his mind's eye: her slim brown hand as it handed him the full glass of cinnamon- and cardamom-spiced milk; the shape of her body as she labored over the fire to make their meal; her arm jangling with bangles as she brought him the dinner plate arranged with delicious food; her face with its large, dark eyes, and the tiny dimple at the corner of her lips as she smiled at him in the morning while giving him a warm honey ginger drink. The more Mardana thought about her, the more his senses were inflamed, and the more agitated he became.

How much have I missed by following Nanak these many years? What have I got in return for following him, hungry and weary, for thousands upon thousands of miles, up and down steep cold mountains, through hot and windy deserts, over stormy seas and flooded rivers and under thunderous skies? What do I have except an imperfect and chimerical wisdom? Wisdom is a poor substitute for real life, for simple human pleasures and joy. One doesn't live forever, and the purpose of life is not some insight that comes and goes like fairy dust in the eyes of deluded fools. Baba talks about vague, intangible things, and I want certainties now, a life where the senses are fulfilled and at rest. Perhaps an ascetic life suits Baba Nanak, but I have had enough!

Sitting up, Mardana broke off a stalk of bamboo and peeled it to get to its edible heart. Chewing on the tender shoot, Mardana wondered why he followed Baba like a meek lamb. *Lambs always get slaughtered in the end*, he thought.

Baba's music and voice have entrapped my soul, and I can't break away from the spell! Mardana stopped chewing as this thought flashed through his mind. Rage rose in him like a whirlwind. *I have been cheated out of life by this magician!*

It seemed to Mardana that for the first time in his life he understood with perfect clarity what he must do: break away from Baba and leave, never to return. He looked at Baba sleeping peacefully; he looked at his satchel that contained the quills, ink, and book in which he, Mardana, had written down

Baba's songs in painstakingly neat handwriting; he looked at the rabab, leaning against a boulder, the intricate mother-of-pearl inlays around its sound hole shining in the moonlight. In his fury he wanted to pick up the instrument and dash it to pieces on a boulder.

Mardana saw the dense jungle surrounding the small clearing in which they rested and was momentarily afraid at the thought of leaving, but his desire for freedom pushed the fear away.

Enraged by Nanak and his rabab, Mardana stood up, turned, and walked away, determined not to look back upon the causes of his frustration.

He walked with one clear intention—to get as far away as possible as fast as he could. Mardana forged ahead, re-creating in his mind the amorous night with Fatima. He was raging and he was angry at nature, *kudrat*,[5] that gives a man desires only to thwart them.

When he quieted down enough and looked back, so many trails led away from him that even if he had wanted to return, he couldn't have found the way. "Just as well!" he said and continued down the same path, images of his longing crowding his mind.

"Yes, I will find a woman now," he fantasized aloud. "Young and beautiful like the first bloom on the mango tree, smelling of fragrant sandalwood and roses. She will be waiting eagerly, her eyes filled with adoration for me. Perhaps her name will be . . . Razaa . . . yes, her name will be Razaa, the obedient one. She will be willing and submissive, unlike my Fatima. I will make a home with her, start another family, and I will never, ever leave. Besides, who knows what's happened to my family in my long absence?"

A pang of guilt held him at the thought of Fatima—her high cheekbones, that dark mole on her chin, her quick and lively brown eyes that flashed in anger or annoyance just as frequently as they did with love and need. "Ah, my Fatima with her sharp tongue, always giving me a hard time about traveling and not being there for her. What a shrew she can be! And who knows what she's been up to in my absence?"

Mardana paused. He clearly heard Nanak's voice in his ears: "*Why should I forget those with whom I have exchanged hearts?*" He looked around, wondering if Nanak had followed him, but there was no one there.

---

[5] Not just *nature* as we use the term, but *Nature*, which includes all there is and the fundamental workings of the universe.

"The magician has gotten into my mind!" He clutched at his head as he fought his way through the darkening bushes. The sounds of beasts roaring, growling, and mating in the forest only inflamed his mind with feverish desire. Mardana thought about all his fights with Fatima and all the things he didn't like about her, trying to pump up his resolve to seek fulfillment with another, convincing himself that his hunger must be quickly gratified. He punched his way through the thick underbrush into a large, circular clearing in the forest and stood transfixed at the marvelous sight before him.

The landscape was completely transformed from the jungle of a few moments ago. Mardana couldn't even tell if it was night or day. Perched on a craggy hill that spiraled up, Mardana saw a formidable and imposing fortress with battlements, domes, and turrets. From its massive iron gate protruded huge brass spikes and hanging bronze bells. It seemed to Mardana that the fortress somehow hovered in the air and was lit by soft lights from both below and above. A valley with a meandering stream and a small village rested at the foot of the hill, in the shadow of the fortress. A festival and a feast were in progress, and enchanting flutes, strings, and drums filled Mardana's ears as he moved toward the scene before him like an iron filing caught in the gravity of a large magnet. Slaughtered goats were being skinned and cut open, and women in colorful clothes were harvesting their organs in neat piles: skins for carpets, water bags, drumheads, saddlebags, and parchment; guts for twine and stringed instruments like rababs and *dilrubas*;[6] hearts, livers, and tongues to be roasted as special delicacies. Some goats, minus their heads, were roasting on spits above open flames. The aromas of herbs and spices and the smell of dripping fat wafted to Mardana's nostrils as he salivated over the scene, his teeth involuntarily masticating over the promised meal.

Wah! Wah! Mardana thought. *This is the place. My heart has come home!*

His intuition was confirmed when several of the women in colorful, sequined *ghagras* and *cholis*,[7] sweet smelling and lovely to behold, noticed him and let out screams of delight, as if they had been waiting just for him. As they ran toward him, Mardana scanned their faces, each one lovelier than the next. His gaze rested on the one who wore a red dress. She smiled directly at

---

[6] Stringed instruments of Afghani origin, also known as Indian harps. The term's literal meaning is "stealer of hearts."

[7] Long skirts and short blouses.

him, and Mardana felt himself drowning in her eyes. Drawn to her without volition, he began walking toward her. All of the women immediately surrounded him, caressed his arms and back, and carried him as if on a wave, into the house.

"*Mardana, Mardana, this is Maya's magic, don't fall into her entangled web! Your ego is creating these illusions.*" Mardana heard Baba Nanak's voice in his head as he bobbed on the crest of the wave. *Oh Baba, stop all this moralizing and let me live!* Mardana replied irritably. *I've had it with your magic and am ripe for some of Maya's now.*

A warm bath awaited Mardana, and the women took turns pouring water over him and scrubbing him down with fragrant soaps. His eyes followed their movements while his heart and body swelled with pleasure and gratitude to Allah for fulfilling his secret desires. His gaze lingered on the woman of his choice, their eyes meeting every now and then, hers coy, his probing. She looked at him submissively, adoringly.

"What's your name?" Mardana asked.

"Razaa."

All of Mardana's doubts vanished. He knew that the reciprocal, bountiful nature of the universe had helped him to manifest his desires. *I have created this with the power of my thoughts! Yes . . . I have learned much from Baba and am no longer the disciple, but a master creating magical realities!*

The women teasingly dried him with soft towels, carried him to a canopied bed, laid him down on soft sheepskin rugs, and rubbed him down with fragrant, heady oils. They brought him the hookah, its bowl full of bhang buds, resins, and other fragrant herbs. Once he had his fill they massaged him and fed him by putting grapes and other berries into his mouth with their hennaed hands. All of them wanted Mardana. Juices dripped from the corners of his lips as they stroked his hair and giggled. He was at the pinnacle of his pleasures; his every desire had become flesh, all because he had stumbled upon the truth about the power of his own will.

In a moment he sketched out his future. One of the adjoining huts would be his own little home, his corner of the universe. It would be comfortable, not lacking in provisions, and Razaa would be there to service his every need. She would be sweet and compliant, like Fatima early in their marriage, before she aged and became more willful and sharp tongued. The lord or lady of the fortress would recognize his greatness as a singer and a rabab player, make him a court musician, and honor him with a small kingdom. He would lack for nothing for the rest of his life.

The women continued to dress him, and then put a chain around his neck. The chain felt tight and heavy. *Never mind*, he thought. *Let them have their way with me!* The perfume they put on him seemed to have a whiff of something like the urine of sheep or goats, but Mardana ignored the smell. Their singing, too, seemed like it had turned from mellifluous to cacophonous, like the agitated bleating of goats before slaughter. Perhaps he had overhead them slaughtering one for his dinner tonight. He was ravenous and couldn't wait to eat.

Mardana recalled a feast he'd had in Emperor Babar's tent once, long ago. Just the thought of it made him salivate: A plump, whole, roasted goat was brought in on a silver platter with carrots, peas, and potatoes garnished with roasted almonds, fried cashews, and raisins. There was fragrant basmati rice and all sorts of condiments and fruit. Mardana had torn off the leg of the goat and eaten it. Babar's musicians had given him some bhang, and the drug had made the food taste a hundred times more delicious. Babar knew how to treat his musicians, unlike Baba, who wanted his minstrel to feed on air. *Bhugat gian!* Mardana scoffed. *For food, wisdom.*

Enough of poor asceticism! God himself gave humans these appetites, he reasoned.

The alluring and mischievous women put a crown of flowers on his head, put vermillion on his forehead, and raised him from the bed he lay upon. Mardana got up a little awkwardly, his heart filled to bursting with gratitude as he prepared to impress the women with his voice. He wished he had his rabab, but his voice alone was beautiful in its range and richness. Mardana opened his mouth to produce a soaring celebratory sound, but his voice came out raspy and hollow. He tried again, and again he heard a very strange bleating coming from his mouth. The girls were laughing hysterically, urging him to sing louder. He tried once more to burst into song, but what issued from his mouth was a high-pitched and vibratory "Mainnn . . . mainnnn . . . mainnn."

The women continued laughing. Mardana was dreadfully confused. What was happening? Why was he standing on all fours? He looked down at his feet and saw hooves at the end of thin, hairy legs; he looked up and saw that the women stood far above him instead of at eye level. Through the corners of his eyes he saw the flapping of long ears, and when he squinted, he saw twisted white horns on top of his head. "Am I hallucinating from the drugs? What is happening?" he tried to ask, but all he heard was a frenzied bleating and the answer of roaring laughter from the women as they danced around him in glee. One of the women stroked his neck and pulled at the rope around it. In a flash of insight, Mardana understood that he was the goat he had hoped to eat for dinner!

"Oh, what a handsome sacrifice he will make!" Razaa said. "Even his bleating is different, sweeter than the others. He will be my gift to Nur Shah. She'll be so pleased she is sure to fulfill my heart's desires!"

"Sacrifice?" bleated Mardana. But the women couldn't hear him. Singing and dancing, they led him out of the house and into the backyard. They opened an iron gate and led him into a dank, dark pen. Immediately, a strong and offensive odor assaulted his nose.

When his eyes adjusted to the darkness he saw other goats, all tied with short tethers to stakes in the ground, staring at him in silence. When they tied Mardana to a stake with four other goats, they all let out a cacophony of bleating. Mardana joined in and bleated fruitlessly for hours, until sleep mercifully overtook him and he sank to the ground, wet and dirty with his own excretions. As he drifted off to sleep, he heard Guru Nanak's words reverberating in his mind: *"O man, weep and mourn; the priceless soul is bound and driven off."*

CHAPTER 2
Rabab

Before opening his eyes the next morning, Mardana prayed the events of the previous day had all been a bad dream. He hoped to find himself in the fresh, fragrant forest with Nanak, to hear him say "Mardana, rabab chhaid, bani aee hai." (Awaken the rabab, Mardana, bani is coming.)

How happy—no, ecstatic—he would be with bamboo stalks to eat, cool, fresh water to drink, and even the hard ground to sleep on under the free and open sky! At least with Baba he was a human, not an animal.

But when he opened his eyes, the stench of the pen and the chorus of loud wails, whines, and whimpers in agitated goat speak, which had begun to make sense to his goat brain, was all around him.

As Mardana listened, it became clear to him that all the goats in the pen were males who had been driven by their discontent, desire, and lust. The women, enchantresses whose spells almost no man had ever escaped, preyed upon precisely this weakness in men. One name, uttered in fear and awe, caught his attention: Nur Shah, High Priestess of Maya, the Goddess of Illusions. Mardana gathered that Nur Shah was a heartless ogress, beautiful in the extreme, who ate men after transforming them into goats. Several men-turned-goats were slaughtered in her temple early every morning; Nur Shah presided over each sacrifice, drinking and bathing in their blood and eating their hearts and brains. Their skulls and bones were kept as trophies or carved into exquisite jewelry.

Most of this information was given to Mardana by a handsome black goat with shining, shaggy fur and majestic spiraled horns. He appeared to be the leader of the goats on account of his size, his beauty, and the distinction of being the only one who had resisted the charms of the subordinate enchantresses and had been changed into a goat by Nur Shah herself.

The descriptions of the sacrifices were rumors generated by ignorance; none of the goats had ever returned to tell. Mardana understood with horrifying clarity that he was here to die. He knew that it could happen any morning, for each sacrifice was performed at dawn, and it was now evening.

What did death mean? Mardana's brain could not encompass the idea. Never to see, touch, or feel, never to see his wife and children, or his dog, Moti, ever again! Never to make music with Nanak! Bleating pitifully, Mardana tugged at his rope to escape. But though his neck was chafed raw by his struggle with the tight string around it, the stake did not budge.

The black goat, called Taakat, laughed at Mardana.

"No one has ever escaped. Know that."

There was finality about the words, like the sound of a door shutting.

"How long have you been here?" Mardana asked Taakat.

"You mean how long do you have? I've been here longer than the others because Nur Shah delights in tormenting me. But you may have longer since you are skinny. They like to sacrifice fattened goats."

Mardana suddenly felt grateful that he had rarely had his fill of food in Baba's service.

"But when the need arises, as during full moons and festivals," Taakat resumed, "they don't care what kind of goat they sacrifice. They'll feed skinny goats bags of salt to make them thirsty so they'll drink a lot of water and look fat and pleasing to the goddess. The slaughter of all the goats from one pen—and there are many pens—takes place on every full moon. On the next full moon, I think it is our turn."

This information made Mardana swell the chorus of complaints in the pen with his own grievances. He swore at Allah for making a cruel and unjust world in which humans suffered meaninglessly. Nanak had said suffering brings you closer to God, but on this earth, suffering only brought you closer to death. He wished he had stayed at home and not allowed himself to be persuaded to accompany Baba on his dangerous adventures. The only reason Mardana had accompanied him was because Baba had promised him riches. How could he have known that by riches Baba meant spiritual wealth and wisdom?

Even in the midst of his rage, Mardana knew that this was not the whole story. It was the damn rabab that was to blame. When Baba came to his door that day and said, "*Bhai*,[1] get ready for a journey," Mardana had made excuses: "Fatima is not well; I am having trouble with my son, Shehzada; my parents are aging," and on and on.

But Baba had walked over to the rabab standing in the corner of his room and strummed it randomly. Instantly, all the chatter in Mardana's head stopped. Only the intangible, silent vibrations from the rabab remained, unfolding vast spaces in his heart where his fledgling soul stirred its damp and untried wings.

The memory of that moment brought some light into the dank, dismal pen and Mardana's darkening brain, and he stopped blaming Baba and the rabab. He shut his eyes and began to hum, which soothed his soul. The other goats had never heard a goat humming before. In their misery, they were drawn to the vibration and asked Mardana what he was doing.

"I am . . . used to be . . . a singer and a rababi," Mardana said.

"Tell us," they pleaded, eager to be entertained with a biography.

"Music came naturally to me," Mardana began, finding comfort in recalling his memories. "It was in my blood. We were Muslim *mirasis*[2] and came from a long line of musicians. I don't remember when I first saw or played the rabab; I feel like I was born playing it. Only dim memories of my grandfather giving me a lesson or two survive. Even as a child, I played and sang secular songs with the family troupe at births, weddings, deaths, and festivals. My fingers flew over the strings, and I never had to think about playing it.

"Playing the rabab wasn't exciting for me when I was young; it was just something we did for a living. I remember the day when the rabab first filled me with wonder and awe. I was ten years old. I remember it well because it was the day Baba Nanak was born. Our village, Talwandi,[3] was full of joy. Tripta, blessed woman, Mehta Kallu's wife, had given birth in the early morning, and the entire village knew of it."

---

[1] Brother, both literal and as an honorific title; also an expression of affection between equals.

[2] Minstrels. The women in *mirasi* families were not musicians.

[3] Talwandi is called Nankana Sahib (now in Pakistan) in honor of Guru Nanak's birth.

"Who is Baba Nanak?" the goats asked in unison.

"You will know who he is at the end of this story," Mardana said, his eyes tearing up at the memory of Baba asleep on the forest floor, his arm for a pillow.

"It was the middle of April. The weather had turned warm, the winter wheat harvest had come in, but I was sad and depressed. I always lived too far inside myself, in my thoughts and confused feelings. I have always been a depressed sort of person, not in the habit of happiness. When others laughed, I wondered what there was to laugh at; when boys played rowdily, or splashed about in the village pond, I envied them. I didn't have a childhood, for my father died when I was still a baby and my widowed mother was busy cleaning people's houses and utensils in exchange for food. I had to take care of my younger siblings and learned responsibility at an early age. I thought others had all the fun, while I alone was locked inside a dungeon, inside my own darkness. The evening before Baba's birth, my depression grew denser till it seemed it would crush me whole.

"But surprisingly, I slept well and awoke early, which was very unusual for me, for I liked to sleep late. I looked out the window to discover it was still dark outside, with the full moon shining brightly. I was fully awake and went out into the fields under the steel blue sky; I felt I had never seen such a morning before. When the sun came up and everything was flooded with light, I felt the darkness within me suddenly dispelled.

"I returned home from the field with lightness in my heart. I also remember the day because when I skipped into the courtyard, I smelled *biryani*. Mehta Kallu had showered money on my aunt, Daulatan Masi, the midwife who was present at Baba Nanak's birth. We were too poor to have *biryani* often, and I loved it."

"What is it?" a goat asked.

"Rice cooked with goat meat," Mardana replied without thinking. The goats set up such a wailing at this image that Mardana had to distract them by continuing his story. "I could tell you the story of Daulatan Masi, too, and a very strange story it is. She is completely mad now; but I will tell that tale later.

"In the first few days after Nanak's birth, Daulatan Masi was full of stories about how Nanak had not wept like other infants at the moment of his birth, but laughed; how Hardial, the astrologer who came to make the baby's astrological chart, exclaimed, 'He will be a unique king, holding sway over vast dominions and adored by all sections of humanity. His name and fame will spread far beyond the confines of India, and his memory will be immortal.' He then fell to the floor and worshipped the child.

"After eating the *biryani* I went into the family room and picked up my rabab. It seemed to me that I had never looked at it before: its short-necked, pear-shaped body that my grandfather had whittled and fashioned from a gourd; its round sound hole covered by parchment; its shiny, round, curved back polished with oil and etched with arabesques and calligraphy; and the taut bow arched by horsehair. I felt great love for this thing that looked like a boat to me, like something that would take me on a life-transforming adventure. But I didn't know then how a wooden thing with strings would determine my destiny.

"As I surveyed my rabab, a great desire arose in my heart to own a more sophisticated rabab someday, the kind I had seen with a wandering minstrel, deeply resonant, made of wood and steel rings, its back, front, and neck inlaid with intricate designs."

At this point in the narrative, the great jumble of Mardana's feelings caused him to break down and weep, his whole body heaving in spasms of emotion. A great pain arose in his heart at the thought of the rabab he had left leaning against the boulder where Baba slept. In danger of drowning in his sorrow, Mardana steered himself back to his memories.

"I kept seeing the rabab of my desires in my dreams. In a king's court, a rababi is playing a lovely rabab studded with gems. When I look at the rababi's face, it is me! Everyone in the court is clapping and saying 'Wah! Wah!' and the king gives me a robe, an embroidered cap, and a silk bag full of gold coins. I had the same dream last night, only the hands of the rababi were hooves."

The black goat laughed and the others joined in.

"I heard about Nanak long before I met him," Mardana continued. "The entire village was abuzz with stories of his childhood. I remember when a Muslim *pir*,[4] who had heard of Nanak's birth, traveled far to see him. He brought with him two small clay bowls filled with milk, one in each hand. He wanted to see which one the infant would place his hand upon. If Nanak

---

[4] A Muslim holy man; also used commonly for any holy man.

chose the one in his left hand, it would mean he would be a guru of the Hindus; if he placed his hand on the bowl to the right, he would be a prophet of the Muslims. Nanak put both his hands on both of the bowls at the same time, and tears came to the *pir*'s eyes, for he knew then that Nanak would be a guru to both."

"How can this be?" a white goat listening to Mardana's narrative suddenly broke in. "You are either a Muslim or a Hindu."

"You have to belong somewhere!" whined Rondoo, a droopy grey goat.

"If Nanak was born a Hindu, he is a Hindu!" the white goat, named Sidda, said firmly. "He belongs in the religion and caste he came from!"

"Baba is neither. When asked what religion he is, he says, 'What religion is the wind? What caste is the earth, sun, or moon?'"

All the goats broke into an agitated argument with Mardana; all except Mannay, a dappled brown and white goat, who stood by silently and listened.

"Baba Nanak began to visit our home when he was around four or five with his older sister, Nanaki; for what do children know about class and caste and religion? *Mirasis* have always been considered low caste, and Muslims are even lower. Nanak himself was born into a *bedi* family: *Kshatriyas*, warriors who also studied holy texts. One day, little Nanak walked over to the rabab, put his tiny fingers on the strings, and strummed and struck it. The sound opened

doors in my mind and vibrated in my being. My senses and soul sprang alive with a mysterious feeling, fleeting as a feather in the wind, yet strong enough to have endured the entire length of my life. At that moment I felt I could do anything, become anything, even an angel."

"Or a goat," interjected Taakat, garnering much laughter.

"Yes, even a goat," Mardana humbly concurred. "As Baba warns, anything is possible on this journey. When Nanak's tiny fingers strummed the strings, my soul sprouted wings, and like a *farishta*,[5] I soared into blue, light-filled spaces with a vision of the earth and all its troubles far below. The vibrations were like a bridge that connected something dimly known to something deeply unknowable.

"Nanak came often to my house and would always go straight to the rabab. As we grew older, we began to make music together. I still remember Baba's voice before it broke: feminine and full of longing."

Mardana went into a trance, and remembering Baba Nanak evoked images of him. There he sat singing under a tree, cross-legged, a *loee*[6] around his shoulders, his hair falling in curls around his intense, passionate face with its newly sprouting beard, his eyes closed as if transported with the first uttered note into God's luminous heart. As Baba's youthful voice resounded in Mardana's mind, he realized that this was what Baba meant when he said remembrance can conjure absent things and make them present.

"Tell us the rest of the story," a voice broke into his trance. With difficulty, Mardana steered his consciousness back to the goats and resumed.

"Baba would come nearly every day, get into a meditative pose, and start the *alaap*.[7] I would recognize the *raga*[8] from his second or third note and begin to improvise on my rabab. Soon I was like pliable clay in the potter's hands, willing, submissive, and entirely under the spell of Baba's voice. It flowed like a river of music from some deep spring within him, unstoppable, sweet, quenching all my thirst, feeding my sadness, and calming my burning brain. As time went on, in addition to accompanying Baba on the rabab, I began to harmonize my voice with his. Sometimes when we played and sang together

---

[5] An angel.

[6] A shawl worn by men.

[7] Sung at the beginning of a *raga*, an improvised, slow, nonrhythmic exposition of the *raga* in Indian classical music.

[8] Meaning "color" or "hue," a melodic mode in Indian classical music of five or more notes upon which various melodies are improvised.

it seemed that our voices, the sound of the strings, and the wind were all one voice, coming from and spiraling back into the heart of the universe.

"Then one day, many years later, Baba came to me after he died and said, 'Mardana, get ready for a journey . . . '"

"Wait, wait. He died and returned?" The goats asked in unison.

"Yes, but that is another story."

"I want to hear that story, too," Mannay said eagerly.

"After this one or I'll get confused," Mardana replied.

———

"SO, ABOUT A MONTH AFTER he died and reappeared, Baba came to me and said, "Bhai, get ready for a journey." I made many excuses, but Baba did not need to convince me with arguments. All he did was touch the strings of the rabab in his special way, and all my resistance melted away. I was ready to follow him to the ends of the earth.

But I wished I had a better rabab, even though Baba's voice and my virtuosity more than made up for any deficiency in our homemade instrument.

"Mardana, we need to get you a sturdier instrument for our journey, one carved of wood and made with steel rings." Baba echoed my thoughts even as I was thinking them.

Soon thereafter, we met a man in the bazaar who asked me what I was carrying on my shoulder.

"A rabab," I replied.

"It looks nothing like the rabab my master has," the man replied.

"What sort of rabab does your master have?" Baba asked.

As the man described it, I stood still, my heart pounding with anticipation. His description perfectly matched the rabab of my dreams!

"Who is your master?" Baba asked the man.

"Bhai Phiranda of the village Bharoana."

"Where's the village?"

"Southwest of Sultanpur."

When the man moved on, Baba said to me, "Go to Bharoana and see if Bhai Phiranda will sell it."

"But where will we get the money for it? It must cost at least five—or even ten—rupees!" I exclaimed.

"Ask Nanaki. She will give it to you."

When I went to Bebe[9] Nanaki, she greeted me lovingly, and when I mentioned money for the rabab she handed it to me without any hesitation. What an angel she is! So loving and kind; a saint, if you ask me. She goes through the days as if she has transcended life on earth and resides in some other realm, looking at everything from a height the rest of us can't see or guess, seeing and hearing things beyond the ken of mortal eyes and ears.

All the way to Bharoana I vacillated between euphoria and despair. The rabab will cost more than I have; Bhai Phiranda won't want to part with it; he might even turn me away from the door.

But Bhai Phiranda was very warm. He welcomed me at the door, fed me, and then asked me why I had come. I came to the point at once. I told him I had money in my pocket and that I would like to buy his rabab. My heart sank when Bhai Phiranda said, "It's not for sale. I am keeping it for its true owner."

"Who is its true owner?" I asked.

"I don't know. I will know him when I see him."

He obviously didn't see the true owner in me, so I said, "I'm here to buy it for Baba Nanak."

"Describe him to me," Bhai Phiranda said.

I described him physically, but Bhai Phiranda said, "More." So I told him the miraculous stories of his childhood. He listened with rapt attention. Later . . .'

⊰•⊱

"Tell us the stories of his childhood!" Mannay interrupted.

"Skip them!" said Taakat. "Why should we listen to impossible stories about some saint? They are probably full of unbelievable miracles. We are all going to die, and no miracle can save us. Tell us a real story to entertain us, for that is all that stories are good for."

"But I want to hear them," Mannay said. "If we don't believe in miracles, we are doomed for sure."

"There are many wondrous tales about Baba Nanak's childhood," Mardana replied, "but I will tell them after this one."

⊰•⊱

---

[9] A respectful honorific, comparable to "lady" with connotations of "mother."

"AFTER BHAI PHIRANDA FINISHED LISTENING to the stories of Baba, he fell silent. And then he said to me, "Mardana, return to your master."

"Can I take the rabab?" I asked.

"No," he replied.

"Can I buy it?"

"No."

I asked him if I could at least see it, and he agreed. When he brought it out, wrapped in a silk bag like a holy object, I saw my dream in his hand. I had a clever thought: if he would let me play it, he would be convinced I was its true owner. I asked him and he reluctantly consented. As I held it, my fingers itched to truly possess it. I sang one of Baba's shabads: "Aakhaan jeevan visrai mar jaoon." (I sing of You and I live; I forget You and I die.) I poured my body and soul into playing it. My voice dripped with longing, my heart swelled with feeling, my fingers were quick and my bow nimble. I proudly displayed my virtuosity. My voice flew on the high notes like a bird in flight and reverberated on the low ones like a flute. I was good; I was so very good, and I knew it. Even before the last note faded into silence, Bhai Phiranda had tears in his eyes. I felt sure that he would give me the rabab as a gift, or at least let me buy it. But no, he still sent me away. I was very upset the whole way back. When I returned to Baba empty-handed, he smiled and said nothing.

A few days later, as I was coming out of my house, I saw Bhai Phiranda, dressed all in white, coming toward me, cradling the rabab wrapped in silk. My heart soared—he had changed his mind! He was coming to give me the rabab personally! I smiled happily, but Bhai Phiranda walked past me. He went straight to Baba's house, and I followed him. Baba had just come out into the courtyard after a bath, and Bhai Phiranda went to him, laid the rabab at his feet, and bowed low.

Baba sat down on his *manji*[10] and unwrapped the rabab lovingly. His newly washed hair shone in the sun as he turned the instrument in his hands. He shut his eyes, put his palm on the strings, and seemed to hug the rabab to his body. He sat silently for a while, as if listening to something. Then, with his finger, he plucked the strings and the rabab sprang alive in his hands. Bhai Phiranda and I shut our eyes; the resonance was so deep and its vibrations lasted so long that we could not help but become entranced.

---

[10] A strung wooden cot.

Baba looked at Bhai Phiranda and smiled. No words were said. No money exchanged hands. Bhai Phiranda ate his meal in silence, then left.

Later, Baba handed the rabab to me, which thrilled me beyond words. I had a sense of purpose and felt I was watched over by a generous, providential God. I saw this event as a sign from the universe to follow Baba on his journeys."

———

Mardana paused. "I'm such a fool! I abandoned my precious rabab; I didn't use my superior mind but let myself be guided passively by my appetites, by the one-eyed monster between my thighs! Oh mad, deluded, blind mind, you got trapped by a straw elephant!"

Seeing his agony, the other goats—except Taakat, who stood by and watched them—were reminded of their own folly. They wept and bleated pitifully. When their agony had spent itself, Mannay wanted to know what Mardana had meant by the straw elephant.

"Hunters make female elephants out of straw to lure and entrap bull elephants. Lust makes the large-brained beasts stupid enough to get caught in a death trap. Kabir[11] uses this image in one of his shabads.

"I have sung this shabad many times, but without truly listening! 'Listen! Listen!' Baba has told me over and over. 'By listening you can become like gods; by listening you can conquer death, see the invisible, grasp the unknowable.' But I have been deaf, deaf, deaf!"

"The blame belongs with life, not us," Taakat said forcefully. "Why does it give us desires and then frustrate us when we seek to fulfill them? Life is without reason or purpose. It is a stupid, cruel joke that is played upon us again and again. The best thing about life may be that we die at the end of it."

The goats listened to Taakat's words, for they made a lot of sense to their depressed brains.

"But his desire for a rabab was fulfilled," Mannay said. "Obviously the universe fulfills some of our desires."

"But what did I do with it? Abandon it!" Mardana cried, ramming his horns into the wall. "Oh fool, fool!"

---

[11] A saint whose dates of birth and death are uncertain, but generally accepted to be 1440 to 1518. Over 450 of Kabir's compositions are included in the SGGS.

"Your dream about the rabab came true. Did your dream about singing at a king's court and getting a bag full of money also come true?" Rondoo asked eagerly.

"Ah!" said Mardana, and then he was silent for a long time, a sad, sardonic smile on his goat face. After a rather long pause, he began to tell them another story.

CHAPTER 3
Mardana Finds a Treasure

"Often on our travels Baba Nanak would say to me, "Mardana, rabab chhaid, bani aee hai." We would sit under a tree or the bank of a stream or river, in sunshine or in the middle of the night, and sing with only nature as our audience. Ah, how unselfconscious and sincere my singing was when I knew my only audience was Baba and my Maker. But truthfully, I always had one ear cocked for someone who was listening with admiration and awe.

The new rabab took my playing and singing to a higher level as Baba and I went from town to town, village to village, and country to country singing and spreading the light and sweetness of the Beloved's name. We reminded people why they were born: to love, to praise the Beloved, and to give gratitude. The ecstasy and passion in Baba's voice was enough to draw an audience. There was passion in my playing and adoration in my voice when I accompanied Baba in his singing. My fingers and voice grew strong and powerful, and I was so attuned to the energy of the universe and to Baba's songs that my entire being vibrated and resounded with harmony. I became aware that I played better than I ever had before, the fingers of my right hand bowing or plucking the strings while the fingers of my left hand danced upon the stem of the rabab, my voice refined, equally trained in four octaves, switching from one to the other easily and smoothly. I could sing and play for hours on end. I began to notice the changes our music wrought in the hearts of our listeners, igniting the waning spiritual embers and ashes in their souls with our passionate song to the Invisible One.

My old dream reared its head and the thought insinuated itself into my mind: I really ought to be adequately rewarded for my talent; a musician as good as I am deserves to be the famous court musician of an emperor! My name should be on everyone's lips. "Mardana! Mardana! Mardana!" I deserve to be remembered for centuries after my death! But who would remember the minstrel of an impoverished guru?

Like a seed, my desire for recognition and reward grew within me, sending down roots that wrapped themselves around my heart and my intestines, growing and bearing the bitter fruit of fantasy. I imagined myself sitting before a king, playing to an admiring audience, and winning the award of a thousand gold coins from the queen for having moved her to tears. I imagined living in a small palace with my wife and children, sleeping on silken sheets, wearing gold-embroidered robes, riding in my chariot on my way to sing for the newly born prince. I would be the envy of all the other petty court musicians.

How poor and shabby the audiences in the villages and towns looked compared to the audience of my fantasies! How simple their fare; how rough their bedding! The images of my glory weighed and slowed me down to a crawl as I walked behind Baba, who ceaselessly walked vigorously onward. I soon noticed that I had strayed behind. Baba had disappeared, and I didn't know where I was.

It didn't bother me much, for I thought perhaps this is the Giver's way of fulfilling my secular dreams. I would seek the perfect lord and master, one who would treat me as I truly deserved.

The jungle around me thickened as I walked further into it. Something whizzed past my ears. I ducked and just in time, for something whirred over my bent back as I crouched behind a bush. I peeped through the shrub, and it took me a while to realize what was happening. Savages with naked bodies marked with powders and paints in strange designs and disfiguring tattoos and facial piercings were shooting at me with bows and arrows.

One savage came from behind and startled me so much I fell backward. His bow was drawn, and he was about to shoot his arrow when his eye fell on the contents that had spilled from my satchel. He especially eyed the rabab and a *pothi*[1] in which I had written down Baba's songs after they had poured out of him spontaneously like a river. The savage made strange guttural sounds to call the others to where I lay, frightened out of my wits. Many of these fierce naked men surrounded me and babbled in a language I couldn't understand. They were beastlike, with stocky bodies and distorted features in hairy pudgy faces. Long thin bones and colored stones pierced their lips, ears, noses, and tongues.

They were peering at the rabab and the pothi—they probably hadn't seen anything like them before. I knew my life was in danger, and I had to do something to distract them. I reached for the rabab and ran my fingers over the strings. The savages were so startled by the sound that they fell back, frightened and fascinated. Tentatively, I reached for my bow and ran it over the strings. Their small eyes widened, and their mouths, full of large decayed teeth, fell wide open.

When the vibrations of the string fell silent, they began to scream and shout so noisily that I knew an argument was in progress. I think they were arguing about whether or not to kill me. They gesticulated toward me and my possessions, and some even put their hands with their long dirty nails on my legs and arms, squeezing them as if making a point. After a prolonged shouting match, they seemed to come to a conclusion. One brute picked up the rabab and the bow with the end of a long pole, as if he were afraid to touch them with his hands. I was relieved to see that though he held them as far away from him as possible, he treated them with respect. Another picked up the pothi, while others tied up my hands and feet and strung me on a pole. They blindfolded and carried me, swinging on the pole from side to side like a beast.

It was a long uncomfortable journey, and I feared the savages would damage the rabab and the pothi containing Baba's bani. As I swayed back and forth on the pole, I wished they had plugged up my ears as well, for the barbarians grunted and growled loudly. What a difference, I thought, compared to Baba's melodious voice! These savages knew nothing of the beauty and subtlety of poetry. How dear were words to Baba! How frequently he lauded them in his bani!

To pass the time and calm myself, I began to recite images and phrases from Baba's banis that I had memorized by reciting, singing, and copying

---

[1] A handmade notebook. For the Sikhs it means a sacred book.

them so often. I hadn't paid any heed to their meaning before; but now I did. Slowly, mindfully, so as to savor them and let their meaning sink like rain into the parched soil of my soul, I recalled some of Baba's words and images:

> God, the Arch Writer, wrote one word with his ever-flowing pen,
> the world came to be, and millions of rivers began to flow;
> as He writes, so it comes to be! He writes the drama of our lives,
> then watches with joy. Not only watches, but participates in it!

Wah, wah, I said to myself as I swung back and forth on the pole, my wrists, ankles, and neck sore and in pain. What a drama He writes! What interesting characters the Supreme creates! What stories! Is He watching me now, I wondered? Is He suffering with me now, or laughing? Probably both, I thought. Does He know what is going to happen to me next? Is it all, as Baba says, written in the cells of my brain? Does He know how I'm going to end up?"

—⊷◆⊷—

"As meat," interjected Taakat.

The goats bleated so loudly that Mannay had to tell them to shut up so he could hear the rest of the story.

"My tears began to flow as I thought about Baba. My blindfold soaked them up, but some flowed down my forehead to the ground. After a long journey I heard the sound of drums, faint, rhythmic, and monotonous. I cheered up a bit, thinking we might be passing through human territory and that I might be rescued. I began to sway my body to the rhythm, which helped to ease my pain and suffering. I have always wanted to be a *tabla*[2] player, but as you know, humans can play only one instrument at a time."

"And when you are a goat you can play none," Taakat reminded him. As much as Mardana was pleased to see that his storytelling skills had lured the magnificent black goat into the circle of listeners, he wished Taakat would stop interrupting his narrative.

—⊷◆⊷—

---

[2] A pair of Indian drums.

"MY FEAR BEGAN TO ABATE with the help of the drums. I felt that people who liked music would be kind to me. When the drums got deafeningly loud, my captors came to a halt and untied me. I stood up stiff and dizzy in the stifling heat. Someone undid my blindfold, and smoke from nearby fires got into my eyes and obscured my vision. When my eyes cleared, I saw large fires beneath gigantic steaming cauldrons. I cheered up when I saw a few human beings tied to trees around the fires. I tried to move toward the nearest one, but a savage caught my hands and tied them behind my back.

He took me to another area where a brute twice the size of the others, so big and bulbous that the folds of his skin rippled and flowed around him like melted wax, sat on a raised platform that looked like a stage. He wore a crown of bones around his head and held the large meaty shank of an animal, which he was tearing at with his protruding teeth. Except for his pinhole eyes, I couldn't see any other features, for they were buried beneath the folds of his face.

Beside him sat his mate, wearing a necklace of bones and earrings that looked like the skulls of small animals. Her huge buttocks spread all around her like a cushion. She was also stuffing a large thighbone into her mouth, which looked like a huge, black hole framed with rotten teeth in an otherwise featureless face.

They burped in unison and looked at me so fiercely that I quaked with fear. They motioned to their minions to tie me up to a tree, but the ones who had carried me on the pole began to chatter as they pointed to the rabab, the bow that still dangled at the end of a pole, and the pothi. I was pleased to see they weren't damaged.

The head creature, whose name I later learned was Kauda, motioned to me to play the instrument. They untied my hands and I eagerly reached for my beloved rabab, holding it in my arms like a baby. I motioned toward the pothi and mimed that I couldn't play without it. I didn't want it out of my sight. I thumbed through it as if memorizing something, then quickly put it in my pocket. I was sad, very sad, and it was a sad tune I wanted to play. At the first sounds, the beings stopped chewing and turned toward each other, their tiny eyes widening in amazement. I continued to play, hoping to charm them into releasing me. An almost human expression came upon their faces, and toward the end of my song I saw tears flowing down their blubbery cheeks. The whole audience broke out into such a jabbering, blabbering appreciation that I was overwhelmed at the noise.

The creatures carried me to the stage where the king and queen touched me with their slimy hands as if they were stroking a pet. From their open mouths came such a stench of decayed meat that I almost passed out. At the leader's instructions, a cagelike box was brought before him. My eyes grew wide at the sight of it. The floor, the ceiling, the door, and the bars all looked like they were made of solid gold! And the bolt was shimmering with diamonds! Allah was fulfilling my fantasy—I could live like a king for the rest of my life with a gift like this.

The king and queen were smiling at me and pointing to it. I was certain they were presenting it to me. I thanked the Giver for writing such riches into my destiny. They motioned me toward the box. I knew it was made of gold, for though I have never possessed the precious metal, I have coveted it, seen it, and touched it enough to know it well. I turned around and bowed to them in gratitude. Someone behind me opened the door, and before I knew what was happening, they had pushed me inside the gold cage and locked it from the outside.

Fellow goats, I can't describe my feelings at this point of the story. I wasn't even done being astounded at my good fortune when a dreadful realization hit me: I was their singing bird in a golden cage. As the days went by, they showered me with gifts and often reached their chubby fingers inside the bars to pet me. They hung a gold-framed mirror studded with jewels in my cage; they brought me exotic fruits, which I ate with pleasure for I had gone without food for a time while in search of my dream; they fed me meat, which I relished, tearing off the fat and chewing it. They brought beautiful clothes, which fit me well, a turban embroidered with emeralds and diamonds, and a pair of well-made, comfortable shoes studded with rubies.

If I could find a way to escape with this treasure, if I could carry away my turban, shoes, and the mirror, I would be rich beyond imagining, I thought. I have always wanted to own an acre of land by a stream or river. With this wealth I could buy hundreds of acres, a large chunk of adjoining land for Baba, a house for Fatima, and servants. My fantasies of wealth knew no bounds.

The brutes took me out of the cage daily and put me on the stage with my rabab, while others, including the king and queen, sat below. This could be a time to escape if I could figure out how to get past the many savages who stood behind the stage.

Even while plotting my escape, I was gratified to see the king and queen sit at my feet like an adoring audience. They would weep and laugh and rejoice at my songs. I was often greeted with deafening applause, which was music to my ears.

I also taught the savages to control their primeval, monotonous drumming into something measured and controlled. I showed off my technical virtuosity, which had always been kept in check by Baba, who emphasized feeling, sincerity, and humility above all else.

I forgot to tell you that the brutes brewed liquor from coconuts—not very delicious, but warming and strong like liquid fire. It was my daily joy. Once when I was drunk, I was emboldened to incorporate dance and mime into my routines. I began to use the mirror in my mimes so that I could carry it away with me on the day of my escape.

At first I procrastinated on escaping. After all, I had everything I wanted. I had applause, wealth—even though it was of no use and didn't make me happy— liquor, and renown. Yes, fellow goats, renown! Soon, to show me off, my captors began to invite their neighbors to come and marvel at me. Savages of different races, some lighter than the others, some more rustic, some more sophisticated, came from near and far to see and touch and hear the singing human.

But as the days went by, my soul grew weary, and I resolved to escape. My audience was sleeping after consuming huge amounts of food and liquor after a feast one day. I kept playing my rabab even as I made my exit so that the sudden cessation of the music wouldn't awaken them. I was playing a soft lullaby, but as I moved away I increased the volume of my playing so they could still hear me. I walked quickly until a sight froze me in my tracks.

Humans, some with missing arms and legs, half alive and groaning in pain, were tied to trees with thick ropes. Others, full bodied, were similarly tied.

"What is this?" I asked.

"Don't you know where you are?" one young man replied. "This is the land of cannibals. Run away, run away!"

But it was already too late. The savages were upon me, and soon I was back in the cage again. From then on, they never let me out, even putting me on the stage in my cage.

I lost my appetite and my ability to sleep. Afraid of losing their singing bird, they gave me the choicest cuts of meats, which I refused. I knew that I could live only as long as I played. At first I forced myself to play, but once I had seen Kauda's meals being prepared I got so scared I couldn't sing anymore. I forgot the lyrics; my voice trembled and went off key; my fingers and bow kept slipping on the strings; and my high notes bordered on screams.

Kauda paused as he ate, looking at me. I could see fear in his eyes. He knew he was going to lose me. After all this time I had learned to interpret his expressions fairly accurately. I knew he was thinking in his twisted way that if he ate me, he could become me. He had his minions bring him the rabab, which he tried to play in a crude sort of way.

He shouted something to his minions that sounded to my ears like "Fry him!" I knew he liked his meat deep fried, but because he had already had his last meal for the day, I knew I had till morning.

Fellow goats, I cannot describe to you how that night passed. I burned in the fires of fear all night long. But early in the morning, around three, my thick and forgetful brain remembered Baba. What an utter, stupid, blind fool I had been! My ego had enticed me into a cage and into a scalding cauldron of oil! With the memory of Baba came a refrain from the shabads that began with "Dukh mahuraa maaran har naam." I began to hum it to myself."

———

A long silence followed, and Mardana shut his goat eyes and began to sing in a bleating sort of way. All the goats gathered around him, for nothing consoles the frightened heart like song.

When Mardana was done singing, the goats wanted to know the meaning of the song.

"The Beloved's name is the antidote to agony," Mardana paraphrased. "Grind it in the mortar of contentment with the pestle of charity. Take it every day and your body will not waste away. Wealth, power, and youth are all shadows; neither your body nor your fame will go along with you. O fool, take it every day, it will defeat even death."

"And then?" the goats asked.

"After I had finished singing Baba's shabad, a memory, like a little light, floated into my brain."

———

"BABA AND I WERE JUST about to embark on our adventures. We were sitting by the Beini River on a cloudy, rainy day. I was cold and dying for a glass of something warm and fiery to drink, and I was very apprehensive about the coming journey. My imagination was painting dark scenarios of storms and hunger, of dangerous roads with thugs and evil characters ready to kill us for our shoes. I said to Baba, "Nanak, give me an amulet for the journey."

"What are you afraid of, Bhai?" he smiled. Whenever Baba smiled at me, all my fears fell away, and I felt foolish that my imagination had carried me away. "Fear the Fearless One and all your fears will vanish," Baba said.

"You never know what might befall us on our journey, Baba. Travelers tell terrible tales, and I would like something that will protect me, something not too precious so thieves would want to steal it, something I could wear around my neck, or sew in the hem of my clothes."

"Mardana, I give you the most precious jewel in the whole world. It will not fail to protect you."

I eagerly put out my hand to receive the gift, but Baba put nothing into it.

"You'll never lose it; thieves can't steal it, fire can't burn it, water can't drown it."

"What is it? Give it to me, please, Baba."

"But will you remember to keep it?"

"Of course I'll keep it. Only a fool wouldn't. What is it?"

"It is a word. Made of air, of breath."

"What word?"

"A name."

"Whose?"

"The Beloved's. It's the only amulet I have."

And then he leaned toward my ear and whispered, "*Wah-hay-guru.*"

The word echoed and re-echoed in the chambers of my ears and flowed into my skull, expanding my awareness to include the sky and everything beneath it. It put me in a blissful trance. I wish I could have experienced this state of mind for a long time, but my cursed, puny brain put an end to it by insisting upon asking, "What does it mean, Baba?"

"Listen to the sound, Mardana. Listen!"

But my mind was too impatient, and I asked him again what it meant.

Baba smiled at me and was silent. Later, upon my continued importunities, he explained. "*Wah,* the exclamation of wonder, amazement, and awe, is the only adequate expression in the face of the incomprehensible and ever-mysterious and miraculous workings of the Guru."

"Who is the Guru?"

"The Guru is the Guide of Guides who whispers in our souls when all our ways are lost, and we find ourselves in the darkness with not a star to show us the way. The Guru is the light within us, Mardana, our highest self. Great, great, great is the Guru, without whom we would be brutes!"

The memory of this event felt more precious than all the treasures I was hoping to make away with. The rubies and diamonds were merely colorful stones in comparison.

At dawn I sat cross-legged and chanted with each breath, "Wah-hay-guru! Wah-hay-guru! Wah-hay-guru!" I chanted until Wah-hay-guru became my breath, my flesh, and my bones. I chanted until everything around me—the bars of the cage, the guard, the forest and animals surrounding us, the half-chewed men—resounded with Wah-hay-guru.

Day dawned. It was the time when Baba usually sat down to meditate and sing under the sapphire sky embroidered with twinkling stars. The coolest of breezes lapped at my body, and I felt calm and reconciled to my fate.

Kauda's servants began to prepare me. While some of the brutes undressed, shaved, and bathed me, others poured oil into a cauldron and added spices to it. Because I was their pet once, I suppose, they spared me the torture of dismemberment. They put me in a ladle and lowered me to the bubbling, splattering oil. I shut my eyes and began to recite the words Baba had whispered into my ear on the banks of the river, with the kind of humility that only death can awaken.

"Wah-hay-guru! Wah-hay-guru! Wah-hay-guru!"

Then with a splash, into the boiling oil I went."

⸺◆⸺

The goats let out a collective gasp.

"But you are still here you did not die!"

"What happened?"

"He's lying! This never happened."

"My dear goats, this is the power of the Beloved's name. As soon as I uttered it with sincerity, the oil cooled down, and I found myself swimming in thick grease."

"How can a mere word do this? Admit you are making up these stories!" Taakat shouted.

"Ah, the name, *naam*, as Baba calls it, made of words and air, insubstantial and invisible, naam is the ship that rescues us when we are floundering and crashing on the hard, jagged rocks of *agan sagar*, the fiery ocean that we are cast into from time to time." Mardana said, the door of his consciousness opening as he recalled memories of all the praises that Baba had sung about the Nameless One's name. "Naam, when we cry it out from the bottom of our hearts, conjures from the smoke of our occluded memory the Captain of our Ship, who calms and cools the ocean with one glance and pilots us to safety."

The goats were silent for a while.

"So, fellow goats," Mardana said, "let us shut our eyes and call upon Him who alone can save us."

"But by what name shall we call Him? There are so many names for God!"

"Call Him whatever name you desire or know."

"And how can He save us when we are on the verge of dying?"

Suffering had dilated Mardana's heart and brain, and fragments of Baba's words that he had paid no attention to at the moment of hearing them now flowed into his consciousness.

"When you adore the Beloved, death is not a calamity, but a marriage."

"Clever words, clever images and metaphors, I don't believe them," Taakat said, turning away.

"But what do we have to lose by believing? Only our fear and anxiety," Mannay said.

"True, true," Rondoo said.

"Which God should we believe in?" Sidda asked. "Baba's wishy-washy God, who is neither Hindu nor Muslim, is too absurd for me. I mean, you are a Muslim, Mardana. Isn't Allah your God?"

"The One Presence and Animating Power that lives in all humans, creatures, vegetation, sun, moon, stars, rababs, and goats is my God. Remember, the One who made the universe lives in it and is nearer to you than your jugular vein. He will cool the burning oil of your fear and suffering. Shut your eyes for a moment and call to Him with all sincerity."

"But I want to know what happens in the story," Rondoo said.

"Yes, tell us."

But Mardana was too deeply into his feelings and memories to continue. "Tomorrow," he muttered.

"But tomorrow they may take you away!" Rondoo whined.

"Tomorrow!" cried Mardana, anxiety lapping on the shores of his being.

"We can die any day. I want to hear the rest of the story."

"No," said Mardana, calming down again. "It is because we may not have tomorrow that we must meditate now."

"But we don't have time!" Rondoo wept.

"When you meditate, you enter eternity," Mardana said, recalling Baba's words.

"But how can you just meditate without bathing, without ablutions, without scrubbing the floors, without the lighting of incense and candles and the bathing of idols in milk?" Sidda asked.

"Be still and communicate through your heart."

Taakat moved away with a grunt. All the other goats, after much hesitation about following a method that was without any ritual, stopped bleating, shut their eyes, and were silent. Their breath rising and falling was the only sound in the darkening night.

CHAPTER 4
Throw Away the Bundle

"So what happened after the oil cooled down?" asked Rondoo, who had wondered about this throughout his meditation.

"The cannibals," Mardana resumed, "were so astonished at this event they couldn't stop gasping and gaping for an entire day. Kauda looked at me with trembling and respect. With gestures he asked me how I had done it. I was just as amazed as they were and was hard-pressed to describe the miraculous power of the name to people who had no sense of the soul. I sat and chanted, 'Wah-hay-guru, wah-hay-guru,' and after many hours of chanting, they got it. I also told them through gestures to stop eating humans. After freeing the prisoners and having one final feast of the ones who were too maimed to survive, they sat with me and chanted.

"The cannibals' features appeared more defined as they chanted, and a sense of humanity seemed to gleam in their eyes. It was as if these animals had glimpsed another way of being far, far superior to anything they had ever experienced before.

"Fellow goats, the chanting transformed them to the point that they set me free. They even gave me the turban, the shoes, and the mirror! I didn't have to steal them after all. God had fulfilled my dream. I would have more money than I could count, and all my desires were on the verge of being fulfilled.

"I packed up my treasure in a dirty rag to deter thieves, slung the bundle on a stick on my shoulder, cradled my rabab, and with the precious pothi still in my pocket, I went in search of Baba, whom I adored again.

"I felt that I was wiser than before. I realized that if the cannibals could change, so could I. My desire for fame and fortune had led me into a trap; my ego had turned my rabab—my gift from the universe—into a curse; my songs, instead of being paeans, prayers, and pleadings to the Beloved, became something I did for my own aggrandizement. In contrast to me, stuffed to the gills with ego, Baba's music poured into and out of him from a pure and unselfconscious source. Baba always thought of himself as God's minstrel."

Mardana cleared his throat with a few bleats and began to sing: "Hao dhaadhee vaykaar kaarain laaiaa."

After singing, Mardana paraphrased the meaning of Baba's shabad for the goats.

"Baba is saying, 'I was an unemployed minstrel when my True Master, my beautiful Beloved, called me to His mansion, dressed me in the robes of His praise, fed me the ambrosia of His name, and gave me the kingdom of his presence.'

"So you can see how soiled I felt in comparison with him as I walked from town to town, singing for my supper and looking and longing for my lost companion and friend. My recent suffering with Kauda had torn off the doors of my heart and allowed Baba in. I resolved to become a true disciple of Baba. I would be aware of the traps of *maya*[1] and vigilant against attacks of desire. I determined to avoid the pitfall of discontent and to believe in the intelligence of the universe to provide for me. I would be as pliant to spiritual advice as a reed and as empty of resistance as the body of the rabab, whose hollowness resounded such sweet and soulful melodies. I resolved to eat wisdom and surrender to the Cosmic Will humbly and joyously."

Mardana paused.

"Obviously, I failed to recognize that desire comes in so many forms and colors, else I would not be here."

"What happened to the treasure?" Rondoo inquired.

"Yes, let's get to the treasure," Mardana said, scratching his head with his back hoof in such a way that made the other goats wonder whether he was stalling in order to make up the story.

---

[1] The grand, cosmic principle of illusion; the appearance of the phenomenal world.

"Are you lying to us?" Sidda asked angrily. "You will go to hell for lying! God does not tolerate liars!"

"God made liars and storytellers," Mardana said and then quickly added, "But I'm not lying. It's all in the books."

"What books, you idiot?" Taakat, who prided himself on having read every book that existed, asked.

"The books that haven't been written yet, but will be, I assure you," Mardana said. "Baba is a great man, and many hundreds of thousands of books will be written about him. Who knows, there may even be a book written about me. 'And then one day Mardana became a goat.'"

"Fool, nobody knows the future," Taakat scolded.

"From one perspective, the books have already been written. Baba says the universe exists in God, who is the eternal author of the live, forever-shifting Great Book of the Universe. The past, the present, and the future exist simultaneously in the mind of God. It is we, ignorant creatures incapable of envisioning a world beyond time, who crawl blindly from moment to moment, day to day, lives to lives."

"I don't even think this Baba exists. I think he just made him up," Taakat addressed the other goats. "What proof does he have that the Kauda story actually happened?"

"I don't have burn marks on my skin, do I? I am alive, aren't I?"

Mardana's logic left the goats scratching their heads with their hooves, and he used the moment to continue his story.

<hr/>

"I CARRIED THE BUNDLE OF treasure on my shoulder as I searched for Baba. It wasn't long before I found him. Every time I have searched for Baba after running away, he miraculously shows up. It's as if he waits right around the corner for me to return.

It was evening. The sky was the color of seawater at dawn with liquid washes of orange, red, and brilliant blue. I was walking on the outskirts of a village when I heard a sound—faint at first, so faint I thought I was imagining it—that entered the portals of my ears like divine wine, gladdening my heart and filling me with joy. As I moved closer, it sounded like all of creation was singing—breeze, water, trees, birds, grasses, earth, and stars—

all were vibrating, resonating with each other and with a human voice. Baba was singing, and all of creation was singing along with him.

From a distance I saw a dear, familiar figure sitting beneath a tree. I hid the bundle in the hollow of a tree, knowing he wouldn't approve. I waited for him to finish his song and then threw myself at his feet.

"Baba!" I said when I found my voice again, for I was weeping and sobbing with relief. "Baba, I am a terrible man. Help me, Baba, help me be a little less foolish."

Then I sat and told him about my adventure with the cannibals. When I came to how naam had cooled the boiling oil, Baba went into a trance, and from the way he looked I knew he wouldn't be out of it for a while.

I was tired so I lay beside him and, comforted by his presence, quickly fell asleep.

The next morning, as we were about to resume our travels, I went to pick up my bundle.

"What do you have there, Mardana?" Baba laughed.

"Oh, just some things," I said, casually.

"Let me see," Baba smiled.

There was no help for it. I opened the bundle and the objects glittered in the sun, almost blinding me. I hoped they would dazzle Baba too, and he would let me keep them.

"I didn't steal them, Baba, but earned them by honest means, I swear. You have no idea how much I sang and played to the point of exhaustion each time! I had a horrifying experience to earn them."

"You had a horrifying experience to learn the value of naam, you fool," Baba laughed.

"Yes, and now I can have naam and wealth," I replied.

"Be content, Mardana."

"I don't want to be content. I want to be rich," I said, marveling at my shifting resolves and deep lust for wealth.

"A contented man is a rich man. And he who has no desire is the wealthiest of them all. Throw away the bundle."

"Throw it away?" I almost screamed. "All our dreams have come true! We will buy land and start a commune with this. You can realize your dream about opening a free kitchen for all in need. We will give some to Bebe Nanaki too, who has always been so kind to us. These jewels will make Mata[2] Tripta and Bibi[3] Sulakhni's life easy—and of course, my own and Fatima's. We can stop our journeying now. We can go home, Baba!"

Baba was silent, and I pressed my point.

"And what will happen when we need anything tomorrow? When we are tired we could buy horses; when we are hungry we could eat."

"Don't think about tomorrow, Mardana. God always provides. Listen to me: throw them away, child. They will only bring trouble."

"Throw them away! At least we should give it all away."

"It isn't yours to give away."

I knew Baba would not be swayed.

"I'll go put it in the hollow of the tree," I said, walking toward the tree, pretending to be dejected, for I had a plan. "I also have to answer the call of nature."

I went behind the tree and pried off as many gems as I could with my bare hands, focusing on the large ones. I took my time since I had told Baba I was going behind the bush, and I always took my time with that. I put the gems in my pocket to sew later into the hems of my clothes. My dream of wealth had come true, and I wasn't about to throw it away. I refused to obey Baba in this. He was too crazy and had no practical sense at all. He'd never had any."

⸺◦⸺

Mardana paused, knowing that he would have to backtrack several steps in the story to demonstrate the arc of Baba's divine madness.

---

[2] Mother.

[3] A respectful honorific, comparable to "lady," similar to *Bebe*.

CHAPTER 5

A Good Bargain

"Let me explain what I mean by practical sense. Once, when Nanak was a young boy, his father, Mehta Kallu, frustrated by his good-for-nothing son who only wanted to sing songs to the Beloved and sit with holy men and ascetic wanderers, gave Nanak the task of taking the domestic cows to graze. Well, Baba took them, and while they grazed, he sat under a tree and fell into a trance. The cows ate up all of the wheat in the neighbor's field. I will tell you the conclusion of that story later. Another time—and this happened after Baba was married—"

"Your Baba is married?" Sidda screamed, as if he could bear no more. "And he's a religious man, a Guru? How can this be? A holy man should never dream of marrying! I have been chaste and devoted to being a Brahman and a priest!"

"Then how come you're a goat?" Taakat asked.

Sidda spluttered with rage and fell into a sullen silence.

"YES, BABA WAS MARRIED AT the age of sixteen. Mehta Kallu hoped marriage would make him normal. Baba was born . . . different. He would abstain from eating and drinking, go into trances, and lose consciousness of everything around him. He dropped out of school several times, because as he said, he had nothing more to learn from his teachers. His father tried everything—physicians, an exorcist, charms, and spells. Then he tried marrying Baba to a young girl, Sulakhni of Batala. Soon after the wedding, the bride was sent back to her parents for three years, as was the custom, and Mehta Kallu wanted to make sure his son shaped up in the interim.

Mehta Kallu called Nanak and said, "Son, you have to start behaving like a responsible family man. You are a *khatri*'s son, a warrior and tradesman. The sons of *khatris* do business even if they have a rupee. There's nothing to be gained from hanging out with *sadhus* and *fakirs*.[1] I have bought a shop for you, which you will stock and run in order to make a living. Learn to be a businessman. Go to Chuharkhana, buy goods cheaply, bring them to the shop, and sell them at a good profit. That's the way the world works. If you succeed, I will teach you the profitable business of trading in horses."

Then he gave Nanak the goodly sum of twenty rupees and told him, "Make a good bargain with this. Increase it a hundredfold, and I will help you run your shop."

Mehta Kallu turned to me and said, "Mardana, go along with him to make sure the money is safe. There are thugs about. Also, you will help to carry back the articles you buy. If you make a really good bargain and need to hire a horse wagon, here's some more money for such traveling expenses."

Off we went. Our way to Chuharkhana led through the surrounding jungle, where we came upon some emaciated, hungry sadhus camped out in the open air. They were stark naked, or "sky clad" as that mode of undress was called, and shivering in the cold.

Baba had a long discussion with them on spiritual matters and discovered that their practice allowed them to receive what they were offered, but they were not allowed to beg for alms. They had not received any offerings in a long time.

I pulled at Baba's sleeve to get him going, afraid he would give them the money that I had safely tucked away in my tunic. I was relieved when he got up after a long discussion with their leader, and we proceeded into town.

I was very happy to see Baba buy rice, lentils, spices, cooking oil, clothes, pots, pans, and ladles. When we ran out of funds, Baba even sold his wedding ring to buy more supplies. I was full of hope that he would now actually settle down to a normal life. When we were done, Baba seemed eager to return to Talwandi.

---

[1] Hindu and Muslim holy men.

On our return we stopped where the sadhus were camped out, still praying, still hungry. Baba told me to collect firewood while he collected stones to make a *chulla*.[2] I was hungry by that time and was happy that we would cook some of the supplies and have a little picnic, but when Baba kept pouring rice and lentils in huge quantities into the pots, his intentions became clear to me.

---

[2] A cooking pit.

"Baba, don't. Please don't, Baba. We will both get a whipping from Mehta Kallu." Baba didn't listen to me and cheerfully went about his business, looking happy and radiant. When the food was ready, he served it to the sadhus. Later, he gave them the clothes he had bought.

I ate, too, and that made me feel a bit better, but I kept wringing my hands in fear and saying, "What am I going to do? What am I going to say to Kallu? How are we going to explain what we did with the money he gave us?"

When we arrived near Talwandi, Baba realized the seriousness of the situation. He told me to go ahead while he sat by a pond under an old banyan tree. I ran home and told Mehta Kallu what had happened. His face swelled in rage as he stormed out of the house and ordered me to take him to his son. Bebe Nanaki heard the whole thing and followed us.

"Where is the money I gave you to stock the shop?" Mehta Kallu screamed. "I told you to make a good bargain with it."

"What could be a better bargain than feeding and clothing the hungry and needy?" Nanak said innocently.

Suddenly Kallu's hand swung back and slapped Nanak hard. Bebe Nanaki screamed as if she had been hit. She tried to restrain her father, but Mehta Kallu pushed her away and kept slapping Nanak. When his fury was spent, he fell to the ground weeping and sobbing, hitting himself on his forehead and pulling his beard.

"I had such hopes for you, my only son! You could have become someone! Even Rai Bular[3] thinks you're special, but he doesn't know what I know—that you're an idiot. My only son a moron! Leave my house and go away! Never come back again!"

After Baba squandered his father's money on the naked sadhus and his father threw him out of the house, Baba lived in the forest around Talwandi for a while. Kallu forbade me to see him, but I would sneak away, and we would sing late into the night. Baba loved living in nature under the open sky like the beasts and birds of the forest. In the meantime, Bebe Nanaki got married to Jai Ram, a revenue collector of the ruler of Sultanpur, Nawab Daulat Khan. Sultanpur is situated on the banks of the Beini River and is a five-day journey on foot from Talwandi. Bebe Nanaki and Jai Ram invited

---

[3] A Muslim Rajput, landowner, and proprietor of Talwandi. He governed Talwandi at Nanak's birth and during his youth.

Baba to come and stay with them, where he could follow his heart and devote himself entirely to the Beloved. But Baba said he didn't want to be a burden on anyone and wanted some employment. Jai Ram introduced Baba to Daulat Khan, who was impressed with Baba's learning and his proficiency in various languages, including Persian. He employed Baba in his *modikhana*, which is the royal storehouse. Baba's job was to keep an accounting of the supplies and to sell them. So, at the age of eighteen, Baba began his career as a government servant.

Bebe Nanaki, the long-sighted woman, found employment for me at the same place. Baba and I would work during the day and play music in the mornings and evenings. The amount sanctioned for alms by Daulat Khan was meager, so Baba always gave part of his share to the poor, and he talked me into doing the same, though I would much rather have kept all of my wages.

Now that Baba was earning a living, he called his wife, Sulakhni, to Sultanpur and started his life as a householder. I also called my wife, Fatima, and my children. Baba eventually had two sons with Sulakhni in Sultanpur."

———————

"Baba had two sons!" Sidda screamed.

"Yes, Sri Chand and Lakhmi Das."

"A guru who had that sort of a relationship with his wife! How can he be spiritual?"

"For Baba, every aspect of life is spiritual. Baba has no conflict between marriage and spirituality. He says they are compatible and necessary. God and the world are one; to separate God from life is ignorance and duality. For twelve blessed years Baba led a normal life, long enough for us to forget he had a crazy streak in him. Those were good years, prosperous years. Even his father was relieved that at least his son had a job and could feed his wife and two sons. Baba seemed content with raising a family, with a regulated life of early-morning bathing in the Beini River, chanting, prayers, work, accounting, measuring, and organizing. In the evenings a community of devoted disciples from all religions—Vaishnavite and Shivite Hindus, Sunni and Shia Muslims, and Sufis—would come to Baba's home, and we would sing for them.

"And then one day in the thirteenth year of his employment, Baba's craziness erupted and disturbed everything again.

"We were in the shop and Baba was standing behind the scales, measuring out grain into a customer's sack. As usual, the beggars were hanging around for their share in the evening. Baba measured out twelve *sairs*,[4] and while he was measuring out the thirteenth, he stopped. '*Tairaan*,' he said, and then, '*tairran*,' and then, '*tairra*.' He went into a trance and kept repeating 'Tairra, tairra, tairra, tairra,' as if he had gotten stuck on the number thirteen. As he repeated the word, he kept doling out the grain to all the poor."

---

[4] A weight measure.

"But why?" Sidda asked.

"*Tairaan* in Punjabi means 'thirteen,' and *tairra* means 'yours.' So he kept saying, 'Yours, yours, all yours.' I kept saying 'Baba, what are you doing? Baba, stop! You'll get us fired, Baba!' But Baba was deaf to me, and before I knew it, all the grain and supplies in the store had been given away to the poor who had come running when they heard what was happening. The men took off their ragged turbans and received the supplies in them; the women held out their veils, which were quickly filled."

"And he was fired, of course," Taakat said with a sneer. "What a fool this Baba of yours is! He lets his cattle graze on other people's wheat fields, feeds lazy sadhus with his father's hard-earned money, then is generous with someone else's grain!"

Mardana lunged at Taakat with his scimitar-like horns. Though he was far smaller than Taakat, who was majestic, muscular, and big, Mardana was so quick and so charged with passion that he managed to inflict some serious injuries on Taakat.

"You can say what you like about me," Mardana said, with blood on his muzzle, "but I will kill you for calling Baba a fool!"

At first the other goats watched the fight with interest, for it was a new form of entertainment, but when they realized that their storyteller might get injured, they interfered and negotiated peace.

"You are the idiot!" Mardana raged, even though Taakat had settled down quietly to nurse his wounds. "You haven't even heard the whole story and yet you pass judgment on my master!

"Some stupid fool like you complained to Daulat Khan that Nanak had squandered the supplies, but when Daulat Khan himself took an inventory, the *modikhana* was miraculously full—more than full! Like Baba said, there is no dearth in the Creator's store, but abundance! Baba may be mad, but he is mad for the Beloved's sweet sake."

Taakat wanted to say something, but he was in such pain from the wounds inflicted by Mardana that he remained silent.

"Now, let me tell you the conclusion of the story about the cows eating up the neighbor's wheat. The owner of the field, unbelieving and egotistical like you, complained to Rai Bular, the landlord of the village, and wanted retribution and justice. Now Rai Bular adored Nanak, and . . . "

"So of course he ruled in Nanak's favor," Taakat muttered.

"Shut up!" Mardana said with so much authority that the other goats looked at him with respect. "Hear the whole story first."

"ALTHOUGH THE EYES OF THE whole village were blind to what Nanak was, Rai Bular recognized Nanak as a divine being very early on in their acquaintance. I still recall the look I saw in his eyes once as he gazed at the child Nanak. They were steeped and liquid with love, worship, adoration, and awe.

Rai Bular, instead of sending a subordinate to settle the matter, came himself. Nanak was out, but I was at their house when the lord showed up at the door riding a horse. He alighted and came inside, for he was a friend of Mehta Kallu. They ate and drank together, and I overheard their conversation. "He is a stupid, mad boy!" Mehta Kallu said to Rai Bular. "What did I do to deserve him? He thwarts my every wish! I told him to work in my fields, to make them yield something, and he starts to sing, 'My mind is the farmer, my body my field. I have sown the seed of the Beloved's name and I am about to reap the harvest. It is such a harvest that even eating, taxes, and charity won't diminish it.' I sent him to watch the cows grazing so he could learn some responsibility, but what does he do? He sits under a tree and meditates while the cows eat up the neighbor's field! When the neighbor almost beat him up, he said, 'The True One will bless your field.' Now the neighbor wants me to pay him for his lost crop! At least negotiate him down, and please put some sense into Nanak, Rai Sahib.[5] He's earning nothing and costing me heavily. Tell him to think about his future! Frighten him with dire consequences!"

Rai Bular was silent for a moment before smiling. "Nanak has a destiny beyond our understanding, Mehta. Come, let us talk to this neighbor of yours."

I was sent to call the neighbor, who was still fuming about his loss. He came to Mehta Kallu's house in a fury, demanding the full price of his crop and explaining to them how nothing, not even an ear of wheat, remained in his field after Nanak's cows had grazed in it. "Come see for yourselves!" he said.

We walked to the field. I noticed that on the way, Rai Sahib paused by a large banyan tree and bowed to it. I was curious to know why, but didn't

---

[5] Sahib is an honorific title.

ask. When we arrived at the field, the neighbor walked up and down the road in a confused state, looking around as if he had lost his field.

"It was here, right here, this was it . . . but I don't understand. What is happening?" he said, scratching his head. Rai Bular asked him where his damaged field was, and the neighbor pointed to a field where tall and healthy stalks of wheat undulated in the wind.

While the rest of us vaguely wondered if there had been some misunderstanding, the neighbor kept saying, "But I saw it! I saw the chewed-up field with my own eyes!"

When things had quieted down, Rai Bular sat on a rock and said to Mehta Kallu, "Come, sit here with me and listen carefully, Mehta. Your son is no ordinary human. I had an inkling of it when I first heard of him, then saw him. I always stopped to watch Nanak play with other children in these very fields; as he grew older, I would see him sitting in meditation there, under that tree." He pointed to the banyan, and all of us turned and looked.

It was the same tree he had paused and bowed to. It was an old banyan, with a thick trunk and many aerial roots that had grown earthward from its branches like large columns. Yes, it was the tree Nanak used to play under with his companions, sitting and swinging on its branches as I watched, making sure, as Bebe Nanaki had told me to, that no harm came to him. Bebe Nanaki would sometimes accompany us and play with and protect her brother.

"Last summer," Rai Bular continued, "when I was riding to the village through these fields on a hot, summer day with the sun beating down on me, I saw someone lying in the field. I thought to myself, 'What madman sleeps under the blazing sun?' I went closer and saw that it was Nanak. I wanted to leap off my horse and wake him, but I stood still. Even my horse was stunned into stillness by what it saw. A large cobra, its body coiled and its hood fanned into an umbrella, lay by Nanak's head, shielding his face from the sun's scorching rays. I was afraid for Nanak, afraid that if I moved the snake might sting him. As I stood and watched, I became certain that the cobra was protecting him.

"A few days later, when I was returning, the same thing happened. Once again I saw Nanak asleep in the fields, this time under a tree. Nanak must have taken shelter in its shade, but the sun had moved and so had the shadows of most of the trees—but not the shadow of the tree Nanak slept under.

While the shadows of all the other trees faced east, the shadow of the tree over Nanak had not moved. This time, I got down from my horse and kissed the earth for bearing a son like Nanak. He is a special being, Mehta. Do not worry on his account. Nature itself loves and protects him. Let this miracle of the resurrected field be evidence to you of that."

Mehta Kallu was quiet as he walked back to the village. When we passed by the tree again, Rai Bular told his men to buy the field and build a tank under the tree to commemorate Baba's childhood and to give the children of the village a place to swim on hot days.

Mehta Kallu was quiet for only a few days before he began to rant and rave at his son again. He was blinded by his expectations of what Nanak should be, blinded by his desire that his only son make something of himself in the world. But why should I blame Mehta Kallu for the way he was, when I have been more blind than he?"

Mardana was so moved by the recollection of these stories and by his own stupidity for not recognizing Baba's greatness that he sobbed and wept. The memories of Baba tucked away in the folds of his heart made him feel warm and safe in the damp and dismal goat pen.

CHAPTER 6
What the River Said

"What happened to the gems in your pocket?" Rondoo persisted.
"The story of the treasure is a long one, and we cannot arrive
at it before I have taken some detours. Now that I am telling stories of Baba's
time in Sultanpur, I will tell a few more before I proceed," Mardana said
firmly, determined to have some narrative rights.

"But we don't want detours," Sidda said firmly. "As it is you have confused our
minds by the twisted philosophies of your guru and your own snarled stories."

"I couldn't agree more," Taakat said.

Mardana despaired. Three out of the four members of his audience didn't
like his manner of telling his tales. What if they stopped listening to him?

"My mind works like that," Mardana began, diffidently at first, but gained
confidence as he continued. "It works in a winding, twisted way, in loops and
gyres, sometimes all tangled up like strings enmeshed one with the other. I
can do no better."

"You can if you exert yourself!" Sidda said. "That's what true religion is:
effort of will and hard determination that enables one to tread the narrow,
straight, prescribed path to heaven."

"I don't like difficult," Mardana asserted. He had realized that his demanding audience couldn't afford to choose their entertainment, as he was their

only storyteller; maybe even their last. "I like easy. Baba extols and glorifies easy too and calls the concept *sahaja*, or that which happens naturally and spontaneously, the way seeds germinate, sprout, grow, bloom, and bear fruit. We humans, too, need to learn to live this effortless way."

"Tell me more," Mannay said.

The other goats, who didn't want their stories cluttered with philosophical or spiritual discourses, jumped on poor Mannay, silencing him.

———

"LIKE I TOLD YOU, IN the thirteenth year of his employment at Sultanpur, something happened to Baba. I had spent enough time with him to know that something potentially dangerous was brewing. I couldn't put my finger on it. After the tairra episode there was a restlessness in him, a *tejas*, a brilliant, radiant fire. He had a powerful, haunted look, as if he'd heard a call or a summons from somewhere. It was as if the measured, usual, ordinary life he had been leading in the world of business and accounting couldn't contain him. I was concerned. I went to Bebe Nanaki, who had noticed it too. She sat silently with me for a while and then said, "We have to let him be, Mardana. He is not ours. We cannot understand him. I just know he will be safe, no matter what."

I kept a close watch on Nanak. I went with him wherever he went, like a shadow. My life was intimately tied with Baba's, and I didn't want our peaceful, predictable, and safe domestic life disturbed.

One morning we went to the Beini River as usual. Baba bathed in it every morning while it was still dark outside, and I accompanied him.

A dark storm with thunder, lightning, and pelting rain was raging. Though I went with him—I had to, I was his servant—I wasn't about to bathe on a morning like that, so I just sat on the bank and watched Baba take off his clothes, move toward the river, step in, and immerse himself. My thoughts were straying here and there, mainly to my bed and something warm to drink, and when I looked again I noticed Baba hadn't surfaced. I thought perhaps he had gone to the other shore, which he sometimes did in order to meditate in the cremation ground. I didn't want to swim to the other shore, so I just kept hoping Baba would return soon. But when some time passed and he didn't, I had no choice but to get into the river and go to the cremation ground. Some fires were still smoldering, but there was

WHAT THE RIVER SAID

no Baba. I went farther, but I still could not find Baba. Eventually I swam
back and ran up and down the bank, both concerned and angry with Baba
for being so careless and putting me through such agitation and discomfort.
When I still couldn't find him, I began to fear the worst. Leaving his clothes
there in a heap in case he returned and needed them, I ran to his home and
told Bibi Sulakhni and the boys what had happened. Bibi started to scold
me for not taking care of her husband—as if I were to blame—and began
crying. Then we went over to Bebe Nanaki's. By this time we were all getting
very worried, and the news had spread. We returned to the shore. Baba's
clothes and shoes were still there, but no Baba. Baba's wife, Sulakhni, began
to beat her breast and keen. The townspeople gathered, and even Daulat
Khan, after hearing of Baba's disappearance, came on his horse. He ordered
his men to dive in and search the river for miles upstream and down, but by
midday, everyone except Bebe Nanaki had given up hope. She had a distant
expression on her face as she looked at the river and said, "He is well. He is
in the Beloved's embrace."

But Bebe Nanaki had a reputation for being as crazy as her brother, and
no one believed her. When I picked up Baba's clothes and shoes, she told me
to leave them there. He would need them when he returned.

We returned to our homes. You can imagine how we felt. Though I had
had my differences with Baba, I realized that if he didn't return I would want
to die, too. I swore that if he returned I would do anything for him, even
sacrifice my life. I couldn't bear to look at the rabab anymore; it looked like a
forlorn, sad, dead thing. It meant nothing to me without Baba.

I sat on the bank of the river night and day, near Baba's clothes, strangely
comforted by the flowing river. It stilled my agitation and calmed me. Bebe
Nanaki's presence also soothed me. When I wasn't sitting there, I was in such
pain at Baba's death, only liquor and bhang could numb it. In an effort to
deaden my sorrow, I fell into a dull haze and stumbled through my days.

On the fourth evening after Baba's disappearance, Fatima placed a plate of
food before me, but I had no appetite. Daulatan Masi, who had gone crazy, as
I told you before, was very excited, at first sitting in her corner babbling, then
running out and running back in. While Daulatan Masi was at the height of
her frenzy, a child came running toward our home yelling, "Nanak is alive!
Nanak is alive!"

I ran out. Fatima followed me, and Daulatan Masi followed her, waving her arms about as if she were going to fly off in the air. The child led us to the center of the marketplace. At first I thought the sun had risen and lit up the square as though it were broad daylight. I rubbed my eyes and realized that the light was actually coming from Nanak. For a long time my eyes couldn't focus on him. He was luminous and translucent, as if the borders of his body were barely there. I saw him fade and come together, fade and come together. His eyes, too, were bright, so bright that trying to look into them was like trying to look into the sun. Something profound had happened to him. Everybody who saw him was in awe, struck silent by his radiant presence. For an instant it felt like we were all under the spell of eternity.

Bebe Nanaki fell at his feet and kissed them, a stream of tears running down her cheeks; Daulatan Masi did the same, babbling all the while, clinging to his legs and not letting him move. Bibi Sulakhni, who had run out of her house with the rolling pin still clutched in her hand, stood there with one hand on a hip and said, angrily, "And where have you been? And without telling me! You could at least have told me and saved me a lot of tears!"

All of us crowded around him after a while, asking him what had happened, but Baba, still in the glow of whatever he had experienced, didn't say a word. He just went home and lay down on the bed. After some time, even Daulat Khan came to his house and asked Nanak what had happened, but Nanak didn't say anything to him either. He was in a cocoon, impervious to the outside, like the caterpillar before it becomes a butterfly, still and silent in the womb of the death that leads to rebirth.

Baba lay silently on the bed for several days, a gentle heat emanating from him. When Bibi Sulakhni became angry and started complaining, as if whatever he was experiencing was somehow a rejection of her, Bebe Nanaki ministered to Nanak with a glow on her face, and Daulatan Masi laughed and wept the whole time, sitting right outside the door of his room.

When days went by without Nanak saying a word, rumors started to fly. Some said he was possessed by an evil spirit from the cremation ground, and some said that water had gone into his brain and permanently damaged it; however, his adoring disciples believed he had gone into the embrace of his Beloved, who had given him the ambrosia of His name to drink.

But Nanak himself offered no explanation to anyone. A few days later, still silent and mute, he started to distribute all of his possessions to the poor. His desperate wife called in an exorcist and a priest; the former wanted to beat him with a broom, and the latter gave her amulets to hang around Nanak's neck. But Baba refused it all."

⟶ ⟶

"Did Baba ever tell you where he went?" Mannay asked.

"No."

"Where do you think he went?"

Mardana was silent for a while. When he spoke, everyone craned his neck to hear.

"I think the river was a door through which Baba went into another dimension."

"What is that? How can that happen? There's no such thing." Mardana was accosted with a chorus of questions.

"I have pieced together a theory based on Baba's shabads. I think he stepped into the timeless, spaceless, indescribable dimension where there are no words, forms, color, or matter and met Akal Purakh—the Timeless One, the Playwright of the Drama of Life, the Unseen but everywhere-present Friend and Lover—and fell headlong in love with Him! They merged in union and henceforth, Baba would refer to himself as the bride of the eternal bridegroom."

Mardana's audience looked incredulous.

"You must understand that Akal Purakh is not a person as we imagine Him. In this dimension our puny brains can only think in terms of image and form, body and matter, time and sequence. But you must always keep in mind that this energy and power we call God is beyond all categories and names. In fact, He isn't a He at all. No, He isn't a She either, though he is both He and She—or rather, neither He nor She. Baba says, 'Naar na purakh kahhu ko-o kaisay.' (How shall I say it? He is neither female nor male.) We call Him a He because we are limited by language. God is an energy that manifests as He, She, It, and Thou. But though this energy is not a person or anything like a person as we imagine it, it is much more approachable than a person and far nearer to us than any human can be. It is accessible through naam, prayer, praise, and love. It is accessible because the Mother Father God is us, deep inside our skins and in our organs. Our very cells are made of God. Whatever and whoever God is, Nanak merged with It and the ecstasy of the union was a trillion times greater than the most intense sexual experience. Baba's shabads after his submersion were sloshing with ecstasy."

Mardana stopped narrating and sang a few different stanzas.

"O bumblebee, suck in that fragrance that causes the trees to flower and the woods to grow lush foliage. If the mind within the mind dies, then the Husband ravishes and enjoys His bride. They are woven on one string, like pearls."

Mardana's singing was so full of feeling that his listeners were moved to silence, each touched in the hidden space within the heart where longing for this union, the very pinnacle of experience, resides. Each felt sorrow and sadness for never having experienced it. Even Taakat felt it and was reminded of how he had hoped to find such an experience with Nur Shah. The feeling plunged him into such pain that he could only find relief in derision.

"Nanak died and came back as a ghost," Taakat said, rolling his eyes in his characteristic way, expecting Mardana to pounce on him again.

"Yes," Mardana unexpectedly concurred. "Baba died into his Beloved. He sings of it often. 'Of course I have died, and now I am alive to live.' He says that it is joy to live in this death! Baba's inner eyes tore through the illusion of death and he became a *jivan mukta*—one who is fully liberated while still alive. Henceforth he became fearless. He was drenched in an insatiable and unalloyed ecstasy. The most harmonious and ecstatic moments between man and woman became the only possible metaphor for the highest and happiest emotion of a human in union with the Beloved. Life, living, nature—everything became an exultation for Baba. He saw God everywhere, in everything and everyone."

"So did Baba never speak again?" Mannay asked.

"Several days later he uttered his first words, words that the river had whispered to him: 'There is no Hindu; there is no Muslim.'"

"That's not true!" Sidda spat emphatically. "There are Hindus and there are Muslims! Religion is very real!"

"For once, goat, I agree with you," Taakat said. "Just look around you and see how real religion is."

"What are you? A Muslim or a Hindu?" Sidda asked Mardana.

"What religion is a goat?" Mardana asked. "What religion is a river?"

"No, tell us. What were you?" Rondoo asked.

"I was born into a Muslim family."

"Then you are a Muslim," Sidda said.

"I'm very confused. Which God should I worship and how shall I worship him?" Rondoo asked.

"I think Baba would say, 'Do what you do with sincerity, honesty, and devotion. If you are a Muslim, be a good Muslim; if you are a Hindu, be a good Hindu. And never discriminate against or harm others for believing what they believe. Adore the Beloved in all forms, in everything.'"

"Enough philosophy! Get on with the story of the gems," Rondoo insisted.

"Just one question," Mannay asked. "What do you think he meant when he said, 'There is no Hindu, there is no Muslim?'"

"It was the message of the river. I swear I heard its liquid and rolling sound as Baba spoke those words. Baba had become a mighty river, certain in its direction toward the ocean of God's heart, the river that is always flowing forward and that is already merged with the sea. Source and goal became the same: no distinctions, divisions, or discriminations between this and that, here and there, now and then, Hindu and Muslim. We are all one."

CHAPTER 7

An Encounter with Thugs

"I didn't throw away the gems. Like I said, I didn't trust Baba's judgment on practical affairs. I went behind a tree while Baba meditated and pried loose as many of the sparkling gems as I could—rubies as big as my eyes, emeralds as big as my toes, and diamonds the size of beans. I put them in my pockets, my shoes, and my turban. In the next village I borrowed a needle and thread from my kind host, and by candlelight, when everyone slept, I sewed the jewels into the hems of my clothes. I was afraid the host might see them and kill us to get them, but my secret activity passed without event and we resumed our wandering the next day.

We were on our way to Lanka. I wished we were going straight home so I could unload my treasure, for we were moving through dangerous territory, and the thought of losing the jewels weighed heavily on my mind. The villagers had warned us of thugs who waylaid wayfarers, sometimes even killing them. I wanted to hurry through the perilous terrain, but my attachment to my heavy treasure weighed me down.

Then, the inevitable happened. We were walking past a funeral pyre with four men sitting around it drinking, when the men spotted us. Before we knew what was happening they had surrounded us, brandishing knives that glinted in the light of the funeral fire. I was afraid they would discover my hard-earned wealth and that Baba would find out I had disobeyed him. My only hope lay in deceiving them with my appearance. I had gone out of my way to dirty my worn clothes and to look like a poor, pathetic servant.

"What do you want?" Baba asked them innocently. The thugs were taken aback by Baba's direct question.

"What do we want?" They laughed. "To rob you, of course. Give us all you've got or we will not hesitate to kill and search you."

Baba handed them his *lota*[1] and his blanket.

Clutching my rabab, I put on a little show to misdirect them.

"Please, please don't take away my rabab," I pleaded. "I will die without it!"

The thief snatched it from me and rattled it to see if anything was hidden in its body.

"Is this all you have, you rogues? Don't you have any gold or coins or gems stashed away on your bodies?" the leader asked.

"We do," Baba said. "We are very wealthy. But you can't rob us of our treasure."

I wished Baba would keep his mouth shut. He was endangering our lives. The thugs removed my turban and opened the folds. I was relieved I hadn't put anything there, though I had thought to do so. They even looked in my ears and combed their fingers through my beard.

"Where is your wealth?" one of the thieves asked. Baba broke into song even as the thug started to pat Baba down. "Heeraa naam javayhar laal. Man motee hai tis kaa maal." (Naam is priceless diamonds, rubies, and pearls.)

One of the thugs was looking inside my shoe while the other was patting down my legs, and I was certain that he would find my jewels. Just as one of them reached for my gown, the leader laughed aloud.

"They are fakirs!"

"Yes, we are, we are," I said, stepping away.

"Look at this one," the leader said, pointing to Baba. "A Muslim cap, but the costume of a Hindu yogi. What religion are you?"

"The religion of love," Baba said.

"I hate fakirs. My father was one, wandering about like you, abandoning his wife and children. He died, killed by thugs like us. Before I kill you, it is my custom to sit and eat with my victims. Come and share some food with us."

I liked the idea. I was hungry, and I thought it would be a great distraction—they might even like us so much they wouldn't rob or kill us. In any

---

[1] A metal or clay jar for water.

case, it would buy some time. I was hoping they would offer me some of their wine, too. The whole scene was frightening, with the evil men, their knives glinting in the lurid light of a cremation. I felt some wine would soothe my nerves and help me cope with what was about to happen.

I eagerly put out my hand for some bread and ate it quickly. But Baba said, "I would rather starve than eat this fruit of sin, this carrion."

I saw the head thief's eyes bulge with rage. I whispered to Baba, "Eat it, please." He was going to either get us killed or make me lose my treasure—or both.

"You won't eat my hard-earned bread?" the leader said, playing with his knife. "It is hard work to rob people. See how much time we have wasted with you, and all for nothing. We could have been sleeping in our beds. It is also dangerous work. Just a short while ago we lost one of our team, the one who is burning over there. Some of the people we rob carry weapons."

"So do I," Baba said. "To capture, conquer, and subdue thieves. I am a warrior fakir."

My eyes popped out of my head. What was Baba up to? I was amazed at the energy in Baba's words. We had never carried weapons, though at the moment I wished we had.

They brought their knives close to our throats.

"Show your weapons!" The thief yelled.

"They're invisible," Baba said.

"I think he's mad," one of the thieves said.

"Consciousness is the weapon with which I subdue the demons in my mind that try to tempt me with maya and rob me of my soul. You think you are thugs, but you can't see how you are the captives of thugs."

"What do you mean?" another asked.

"You think you are stealing from other people, but you are only stealing from yourself," Baba said. "You have been given the priceless jewel of your soul, and you are throwing it away for the sake of a cowry! Fools, you are robbing yourselves!"

"Shut up!" the leader said.

"You can hide from the law but you cannot hide from the All Seeing," Baba continued.

"I'm not in a good mood today," the leader of the thieves said. "I have lost a comrade and am inclined to take revenge. I don't want to hear about the stupid soul. What soul? Look at him! He will soon be ash. Finished, over, done with! Ash! Ha, the soul!"

"Your comrade is not dead," Baba said.

"He's definitely mad," another thief confirmed.

"Death has beaten him up, wrestled him to the ground, and is about to crack open his head. Yama, Lord of Death, has opened his ledger and is calling your friend to account for his deeds and unfinished business," Baba continued.

"I'll crack open your head first," the thug said, raising his big knife over Baba's head.

"We are ready," Baba said. "Just make sure to cremate us after killing us, so the soldiers of the king don't find our bodies and accuse you."

Just then, a loud crack from the direction of the pyre made everyone turn their heads toward the burning body. Their dead friend's head fell from the funeral pyre and rolled away, the skull cracking and crackling in a burst of leaping, sparkling flames.

The leader lowered his knife and said to one of the thieves, "Guard them while I go put his head back on the pyre. You," he told another, "go collect firewood to cremate these clowns."

They were gone a long time while our guard played cat and mouse with us, bringing his knife close to our necks, then laughing, pulling it away, and pointing it at our eyes. It was all very scary, but Baba just smiled and said to me, "Don't worry, Bhai."

"How can you be so calm when death is staring you in the face?" I asked.

"Nothing will happen if it isn't our time to die, and nothing can stop death if it is. Rabab chhaid, Mardanaiya," Baba said, using his affectionate variation of my name.

I stared at him, thinking that the danger had finally turned his wits.

"Is this really a time to sing?" I said.

"No better time than in the mouth of death," he said.

So I reached for my rabab with trembling fingers, keeping an eye on the thug and his knife. My fingers were numb with fear, and my playing sounded like screeches.

"Come on, Mardana," Baba said. "Be a Mardana."

"I am not a Mardana, but a Marjana," I replied."

The goats looked at Mardana, confused, so Mardana had to suspend his narrative momentarily and explain the reference.

"Before I was born, my mother lost many children in infancy—about four, I think. Then, when I was about to be born, someone told my parents that the evil eye could be averted if they named me 'Marjana,' which means 'the one who is to die.' It was only after I met Baba that he renamed me 'Mardana.' By changing the 'j' into a 'd,' he turned me from a wimpy 'Marjana' into 'Mardana,' which means 'a strong, brave, and courageous man.' It also means 'Marda Na,' or 'the one who will never die.'"

The recollection of this detail brought Mardana into a silent and reflective trance. He would have stayed in that space for a while if the goats hadn't nudged him into completing his tale.

"BABA SAID, "PUT SOME ENERGY into it, Mardana! Let's sing a last song before we die."

Well, I couldn't get excited about dying, but when Baba began to sing, I calmed down somewhat. I even joined Baba as he sang, though my voice verged on a crazed release of fear and tension. Let me tell you the gist of Baba's song so that when I sing it, you will understand it: "Come, O my companion, let us meet and contemplate and chant the True Name. Let us weep over the body's separation from the Lord and Master and keep a watchful eye on the path that ends in death, for He who creates, destroys; Everything that Is, is His Will."

Aavhu milhu sahayleeho sachrhaa naam la-ayhaa,
rovah birhaa tan kaa aapnaa saahib samhaalayhaa.

We hadn't even finished singing when the thugs who had gone to take care of their dead friend's burning head rushed back to where we sat and fell at Baba's feet, jabbering and blabbering incoherently. Only a few words were audible in all that muttering: "Forgive us, save us; forgive us, save us!"

When they calmed down, the thugs explained what had happened. As they neared the pyre, they heard screaming and shouting, wailing and cries of pain. They thought they were imagining the sounds, but soon they began to see things as well. Dark elfish creatures with big teeth and claws were gnawing on the dead man's bones, while others were lacerating his screaming soul. Yama Raj, Lord of Death, was reading from his ledger and reciting all the dead man's evil deeds, and it was a long list of robberies, murders, and rapes. Even his minor transgressions—like cheating a beggar of a few coins, telling lies that harmed people, behaving cruelly or angrily—were recorded there. Baba had been right; it was time to do the accounts, and their dead friend had come up very short. He now had to pay up his account with untold physical and mental torture. Death was about to drag him away to the sound of cacophonous trumpets when out of nowhere the men heard lovely, celestial harmonies. Angels appeared and demanded the dead man's soul.

"What good has he done that you have come to claim his soul?" Yama thundered.

"None," said the angels. "But Baba Nanak glanced his way, and that is enough to redeem him."

The thieves, who had witnessed their dead friend's torture, held on to Baba's feet and begged him to save them.

"Only love for the True One will save you; the Forgiver forgives all," Baba said, motioning to me to resume playing and singing. Sitting in the light of the burning fire, we sang for the thieves.

> When I have you, I have everything;
> You are my treasure.
> If it pleases you, rivers flow over dry land
> The lotus blooms, man crosses the terrible ocean
> Or he drowns.

What the thieves had witnessed through the open door of death had ripened them for reform. They sat and listened with attention and wept with remorse. Baba sang late into the night about the wealth of love and praise, the treasure of wisdom, the invaluable riches of naam, and the honor of earning a living by honest means and sharing those earnings with others.

I played and sang very well. I was relieved to be alive and still in possession of my treasure. We spent the night with our robber friends, and in the morning we said cordial good-byes and resumed our journey."

Just when Mardana finished this part of the story, two enchantresses came into the pen with lanterns. They put red marks on two goats, sealing their fates. The two had one night to live and would be sacrificed in the morning. This served as a reminder to all of the goats of their own fates. Mardana became weary and insisted upon sleeping, even though the goats reminded him of how little time was left.

"Before you sleep, please just tell me one thing," Mannay asked. "What did Baba mean when he said he was a warrior fakir, that his weapons were invisible?"

"Ah!" Mardana cried. "If we had been warrior fakirs, like Baba, fighting the demons and thugs inside our minds that capture and possess us, our lust would not have landed us in this pen! It is here, here," Mardana said, beating his head against the wall, "that we must wage the war against maya, bearing the weapon of vigilant attention against the thoughts that turn us into beasts!"

CHAPTER 8
At the Friend's House

"Having survived the thugs, I was very hopeful about my future; and whenever I was hopeful, I loved and adored Baba. As I walked behind him in my robe heavy with gemstones, I felt content and sweetly joyous to be his servant, companion, and rababi.

At sunset we reached the edge of a beautiful forest. The people in the last village we visited had mentioned this place with dread, and I wondered why they were so afraid. The sun was filtering through the leaves and everything looked quite serene. But when the sun set, the forest grew dense, hungry animals growled in the night, strange birds squawked and screeched, and jackals and hyenas cackled crazily. As the forest darkened, my mood did as well.

"Baba Nanak, I'm afraid," I said. "Any wild animal can make a meal of us at any time. And I'm hungry."

"Don't worry, Mardana," Baba Nanak replied. "See that yellow light there? That is Sheikh Sajjan's house. I'm sure he and his wife will be happy to cook you some food."

"Sheikh Sajjan! Did I hear you right? Did you say Sheikh Sajjan? Baba, in what world do you live?"

"I've heard he's a good man. He keeps both a mosque and a temple and takes care of hungry, tired travelers. *Sajjan* means friend," Baba replied.

"No, no, Baba, no," I said, digging in my heels like an overloaded donkey as Baba pulled me forward. "Haven't you heard what Sajjan does to his guests?"

"I've heard something. If the rumor is true, then all the more reason for us to go to him."

"You've heard, and you're still putting me, and yourself, in danger? Are you ready to kiss life good-bye? I'm not going. I prefer hunger to death."

"Mardana," said Baba Nanak, putting his arm around my shoulders. "There's nothing to fear."

"Nothing to fear? He robs his guests . . . "

"Our wealth cannot be taken away, Mardana."

"Sajjan doesn't know that! What about our lives? He chops up his guests and throws them into a well. Our lives are ours to lose."

"No, Mardana, not even our lives are ours. They belong to the Power that made us."

"Well, mine is mine. I'm not ready to meet the Nameless One just yet."

"Trust and come."

"Yes, trust like all those rotting bodies in his well must have trusted. No, I won't come with you."

"If you conquer your fear of death while you are still alive, you'll never have to die again. Then the thought of death will only bring joy to the heart, for death is the Beloved's summons."

"Death is the Beloved's summons? As far as I am concerned, this is grounds for abandoning the Beloved, whoever he might be. My beloved, Baba, is a kind woman who will keep me at her breast forever."

Baba laughed.

"Our adventure has brought us to Sajjan's gate. Let us go in and greet him."

"Don't do this to me, Baba," I pleaded. "Don't. Feel how my heart is thumping against my breast. Remember Dulla, our neighbor in Talwandi, whose heart sped up, and he fell down dead by his cattle, his face in a pile of dung?"

"It's your uncontrolled mind that is doing this to you, Mardana. Conquer your mind and you conquer yourself."

I couldn't calm myself, as Baba advised. I continued shaking in my shoes so violently that my bones were rattling.

"If Sajjan is everything everyone says he is . . . " Baba began.

"He is! He is!" I shouted.

"Then he needs help."

"*He* needs help? What are you talking about?"

"His evil soul is calling for help. Everything and everyone in nature is seeking only the Beloved, Mardana. Only sometimes they don't know it, and mistakenly think they are seeking wealth and power or youth and beauty."

"I am only seeking safety and food," I replied. "And I don't want to go to that godforsaken man's house."

"God forsakes no one. Everything in nature is God. There is nothing else."

"Well, I like some parts of God better than others," I replied. "And I positively dislike the part of God that is Sheikh Sajjan."

Baba smiled at me with amusement.

"If it's any consolation, Mardana, I'm afraid, too," he said. By now we had reached the house, which was illumined by a sole light in the upstairs window.

"You're lying. I've never seen you afraid. You are not like other humans."

"Why, Mardana, I am human to the core. I experience everything you experience."

"Even lust and greed and pride?"

"Yes, all those beasts attack me, too."

"Then how do you . . . ?"

"Singing to the Beloved keeps them at bay. Come, sit. Rabab chhaid," Baba said, squatting on the ground by the gate.

Baba was sitting in the shadows of the trees while strange, frightening sounds echoed all around us. I struck the notes and Baba's deep, resonant voice began the alaap with the note *sa*.[1] So deep it was, so steady, this fundamental and immovable note with no sharps and no flats, that I immediately felt calm. If God has a sound, it must be *sa*, I thought. After a prolonged alaap that quelled my agitation, Baba began:

> Jeo darat hai apana
> Kai sion karee pukaar?
> (I am frightened.
> Who shall I call out to in my fear?)

---

[1] The first note in the Indian musical scale.

The primal humanity of the cry struck a chord deep within me. I joined in with a quaky voice and sang along with him. Baba's next lines answered the question:

> Dukh visaaran saiviyai, sadaa, sadaa datar.
> (Remember and serve Him who dispels fear and pain and
> is forever and ever merciful.
> Your name, Beloved, carries me across.)

I felt like a sinking stone in a sea of fear and reached out for the help Baba's words offered. His notes, his music, and his deep, resonant voice were like a boat; I climbed aboard onto safety. Soon the turmoil in my soul ceased with the rhythmic breathing the song demanded.

Our singing alerted Sajjan, who came to the gate, looking pious and sweet and welcoming. Both Baba and I knew it was a sham, but we still went in. Oh, he was most hospitable.

"You want a room for the night? Yes, we have one. Welcome, welcome," he said, leading us into a room. "I have a mosque and a temple for you to pray in. What are you, Hindu or Muslim? I can't tell from your dress."

He looked us up and down, eyeing the sack in which I carried the rabab and the pothi.

"Neither," we replied.

He offered us food. Baba refused, but I wanted to eat well before I was robbed and killed, so I wouldn't be hungry in the hereafter.

"I'd like some *paranthas*,[2] and some *daal*."[3]

"Of course, of course," he said, rubbing his hands together and smiling most smugly.

"And some *halwa*,[4] too," I said, wanting to make my last meal very special.

Sajjan left us, ostensibly to get the food, but I knew he had gone to fetch the axe.

I don't know if fear had turned my wits, or if I was just imagining it, but I felt I had entered Sheikh Sajjan's body and skull and was hearing all of his thoughts.

---

[2] Fried bread.
[3] Lentils.
[4] Indian dessert.

"They don't need food where they are going," he was thinking. "Into the well, my stupid friends! The younger doesn't look stupid, though. He has a glow about him that bespeaks enormous wealth. He isn't carrying anything, but probably has jewels or coins hidden in his turban. That skinny, greedy servant of his is probably carrying something for his master in that big sack. He doesn't look like he would have anything of his own, that sorry, pathetic-looking fellow. I wonder how they will die? I love that look in their eyes when the truth dawns on them: terrified, pleading, whimpering, and groveling. Some instantly bring out their valuables and hope to be set free. Set free! So they can go and tell others? No, no, my friends, no word gets out of here."

I was stunned by my new powers, and a jumble of feelings arose in me. I would have told Baba, but I feared that my own deceit about the treasure had made me Sajjan's brother, that I was complicit with him in my greed, although I hadn't killed anyone to acquire my wealth. However, I was in some sense even lower than Sajjan, having fed on human flesh, albeit unknowingly. I also felt very angry that he thought I was a poor, sorry fellow. I wanted to shout at him, "I am richer than you, you idiot!" But I was also pleased that was what he thought, for it would save my life and my treasure should we escape by some miracle of Baba's making.

"They look like they could be holy men, too," Sajjan was thinking, beginning to have some qualms, which he instantly quashed with the thought: "They could be pretending. A lot of them do, to pass safely through these forests. Even if they are holy men, what difference does it make to me? Muslims and Hindus are all alike. They see a mosque or a temple and they feel safe. Just walls made in particular shapes lead them to my web! Where is their God when I kill them? They are weak, ignorant people who let fear of imaginary gods keep them from living. You have to take what you can. Like my father always said, 'Life is a jungle and each man must fend for himself. Become rich! Make your wife happy! Make your life easy!' I've taken my father's advice and made a good life for myself. I have the consolation of knowing that there is no man alive within a thousand miles with a harder heart than mine!"

Baba had motioned me to begin playing the rabab, but I pleaded with him. "Let's run away. There's still time. I would rather die of hunger and take my chances with the wild beasts. This man is definitely going to kill us. He has gone to fetch the axe!"

"Mardana, please," said Nanak, sitting cross-legged on the floor. "We will charm him with our shabads."

I opened the sack just as Sajjan appeared at the door. His right arm was still behind the wall, and I knew he had brought with him the instrument of our death.

I looked at him as I pulled out my rabab. Sheikh Sajjan looked disappointed—just a useless musical instrument. "But those knobs may be gold. In any case, you never know what's hidden in their clothes," I heard him think.

Baba innocently shut his eyes and began to hum. I felt like shutting my eyes, too, for Baba was making the kind of sound that makes you want to shut your eyes and taste the inner silence it produces; the kind of sound that at once arouses the soul and calms it. But my eyes were riveted on the murderer's every move.

Baba's voice began to work its magic. I could see that Sajjan's eyes also wanted to shut as he stood in the doorway, but he jerked himself awake. The music touched some chord in Sajjan, and he thought, "Let them sing this one song before I silence them forever."

Baba began to sing the shabad that begins:

> Dhaanak roop rahaa kartaar.
> Faahee surat malookee vays.
> (The wild dogs of greed are with me.
> In the early morning they howl into the wind . . .
> Falsehood is my dagger, I eat the carcasses of the dead . . .
> I am deformed and horribly disfigured . . .
> Your name alone saves me . . .
> You are my hope, you my support.)

I was amazed at what Baba was singing—and with so much longing, pleading, and honesty! It was as if he were baring his soul before God, stripping himself down to his human, animal core. As he continued to sing I wondered whether Baba was baring his own soul or holding up a mirror to Sajjan's heart. He sang as if the confession was wrung out of him. As I sat there playing the rabab, one eye peeled back to watch Sajjan's every move, listening to Baba's raw revelations, I knew that the song applied to both him and Sajjan. What Baba had said about being entirely human was true. Baba did not set himself up to be a superhuman; he too contained all the darkness the human heart is heir to, but he had transformed himself into what a human could become. He was aware and conscious of the teeming shadows of his own animal-human soul, and he had transcended them with the help of his Beloved. I now saw how he had made a ladder from the sound of God's name and climbed out of his own darkness. Baba was a man with animal instincts who had become the pinnacle of what a human could be: divine.

In that moment I was not afraid, and my own path became as clear to me as daylight. I too could climb out of the jungle of my confused and ignorant self with God's help; I too had hope. Baba had given it to me. I looked at Sajjan and saw that his greedy, corrupted soul, like a bird trapped in a golden cage of its own worldly desires, was beginning to have an inkling of a freedom richer than its gilded bars. I finally shut my eyes and feared at once it was a mistake, for there was a sudden movement and clatter in the room. I jerked my eyes open, and the first thing I saw was a glinting dagger lying at Baba's feet. I sprang up and clearly saw what was happening—Sajjan lay in a heap at Nanak's feet, sobbing and weeping so violently that his whole body heaved. He was muttering something between his sobs. I couldn't make it out at first, and then I heard the words 'Help me, help me!' As I watched, Baba opened his arms, and Sajjan went into them, crying like a child. Sajjan's wife came running downstairs to see what the commotion was. At first she feared we had harmed her husband and began to shout, but when she saw what was happening, she stood still, amazed at the scene before her, her husband sobbing and Baba stroking his hair. A long time passed like this. I was moved, though I felt jealous, too, for Baba had never taken me into his arms like that. I felt unclean, heavy with my own sins. I also wanted to confess, to rip open my hems. But I refrained. *I haven't killed anyone for the gems*, I argued with myself—they were given to me. *I am not an evil man*, I consoled myself. And yet, none of my reasoning made me feel any better. My attachment to my treasure was very strong. And I did nothing."

"Sudden reformations! What a sham! You can't straighten a pig's tail!" Taakat said.

"Sheikh Sajjan's grief and repentance seemed genuine. He had already begun tearing down the mosque and the temple before we left. I left feeling ashamed of the treasure I still possessed, but not enough to get rid of it. I am the evil person here. I am the pig's tail!" Mardana sobbed.

"Don't feel bad," Rondoo said. "It is only natural to want a good life for yourself. And you are right, you didn't do anything wrong."

"I disobeyed my Guru," Mardana said. "And I suffered for it."

"But you didn't die," Rondoo said.

"I am about to."

"But not for not throwing away the treasure."

"I did die for that," Mardana said, cryptically, as he proceeded with his story.

CHAPTER 9

Stone

"In our travels we came upon a landscape of gentle rolling hills, yellow with flowering mustard, trees for shade, palms with ripe coconuts, sweet, wild bananas, bushes thick with berries, and the crystal waters of a river meandering through the valley. It was a marvelous place to sojourn: no jungle, no wild animals, nothing to worry about or fear. I was happy to have survived another dangerous adventure and come out of it with not a hair harmed, still in possession of my beloved treasure.

We picked the best spot in the valley and settled down under a shady tree. I gorged myself on fruit and in the evening cooked wild rice and vegetables, local herbs, and greens. A dead tree provided firewood. We were both tired, so we made plans to stay here a while. It felt so peaceful lying under the open skies at night with stars so big I felt I could reach up and pluck them. A warm, fragrant breeze caressed my skin as I looked up at the bright and sparkling patterns of the constellations, feeling the presence of God all around and within my happy heart.

The next day was even better. I awoke to a brilliant morning, the river flowing like liquid crystal over jeweled pebbles, gliding and glistening over the boulders. The steady drone of Being, the *sa* and *pa*[1] together, emanated like music from the bubbling river. The comforting sound mingled with the song of a small blackbird whose wings turned to blue in flight, its liquid refrain so melodious that

[1] The fifth note of the Indian musical scale.

passersby would stop in delight and remember the Path to which we all belong and which always calls to us in our dreams and soulful moments.

I remember thinking, *Such a bird is Nanak, my Master, my Guru, my Friend.* I felt tremendous love and gratitude to him and realized how fortunate I was to have experienced so much, learned so much, and felt so much. If I had become some rich man's minstrel, I would have been comfortable, surely, but would my universe have been as vast as Baba's presence made it?

I gave Baba a massage. We prayed and sang, ate, and dozed in the sun. All day I vibrated with joy, wishing I could live like this forever. But how easy it is to forget the volatility of the human mind and how it can turn from this to that in the blink of an eye!

In the evening the caravan of a *nawab*[2] arrived and began pitching tents a little distance away from us. It was a large caravan, with horses and buggies, goats and camels. The tents were made of silk, wool, and fur, and the camp had an air of opulence. Torches and fires were lit and elaborate dishes prepared. The smell of spices and meat, rice and *rotis*[3] aroused my hunger all over again. When later the smell of bhang wafted over to me, I sat up and wanted some.

Now, if ever I have a weakness besides treasure, it is bhang. If I smell it, I have to have it. I'd had it several times before, the most memorable of which was in Saiyidpur during the massacre by Babar, the Mughal emperor. Babar had not even spared the holy men. Baba and I were arrested and put into prison. We were certain our end had come. What a horrible time it was! Baba was so disturbed and moved that songs and music poured out of him. He even rebuked the Beloved in his songs:

> Aytee maar pa-ee karlaanay tain kee darad na aa-i-aa.
> (When there was such slaughter and lamentation,
> didn't you feel pity and pain at the sight of the carnage?)

Oh yes, Baba's relationship with the Beloved included many quarrels. Baba's songs comforted the prisoners, all of whom came to listen.

Emperor Babar heard about a holy man and his rababi singing in prison and invited us to his tent to sing. What wealth and extravagance! The inside of the tent was maroon and intricately hand embroidered. In one corner the court musicians were playing flutes in Raag[4] Darbari, attired in beautiful silk robes and colorful turbans. The tent was full of smoke from the elaborately carved hookahs, and even the musicians were taking drags from them. My nostrils flared and took in the fragrance.

Babar took out a little leather bhang pouch from his pocket, poured a few small, tight, dry buds into the palm of his hand and put them in the cups of two hookahs. He motioned one of his attendants to offer them to Baba and his accompanist. I eagerly reached for the pipe, but Baba said, "I have already taken it." My head swiveled around to look at Baba. He had never taken any.

---

[2] A governor or ruler under the Mughal empire.
[3] Indian bread.
[4] A melodic mode of Indian classical music. All of the shabads in the SGGS have accompanying raags.

"But this stuff is special." Babar said.

"The stuff I have—its effect never goes away." Baba said.

Babar was amazed.

"And all of its side effects are great," Baba continued.

"Let me smoke it," Babar said eagerly.

Baba said to me, "Rabab chhaid, Mardanai."

And Baba sang:

> My heart is the pouch, my love of thee
> The bhang that intoxicates me, Beloved!

I could see how deeply Babar was moved. For an instant, the great conqueror's love of power was drowned in one drop from the ocean of love in Baba's soul. For an instant he forgot his urge to conquer, rule, and command.

The cruelest of emperors was better than me, for I felt no such love. Though I played the rabab very well, my motive was to impress the emperor in the hopes he would employ me. And my attention was on the bhang.

The emperor wiped a tear from his eye and asked Baba Nanak to accept something else. I hoped Baba would ask for something that would make our life more comfortable, like servants, a carriage, horses, or palanquins, or at least a pouch full of gold coins—but what did Baba ask for?

"Release all the captives of Saiyidpur."

"Done!" said Babar.

Later, the emperor's musicians took me aside and offered me the pipe. How wonderful music seemed to me after I had my smoke! How beautiful everything became! My senses sprang alive, and everything was more vivid— the colors of the flowers in the vases, the shapes of things, the play of light upon them, the texture of the sounds coming from the rabab, the gold rings of the emperor, the gold earrings in the musicians' ears. What a wonderful drug bhang is! Eventually, I said good-bye to the musicians and their bhang, and we went on our way.

Now, let me get back to the story of the wonderful valley. The next evening, lying under the stars in the valley next to Baba, the fragrant smell of bhang from the nawab's camp came drifting over to me on the breeze, and I knew I had to have some. When Baba fell asleep that night, I went over to the encampment of the nawab, and one of his musicians invited me to share the pipe with him.

But this time, fellow goats, the drug did not have the same effect. It made me cranky, unhappy, irritable, and upset. I returned to the sleeping Baba and couldn't fall asleep. The life that I had been so happy with just a short while ago became abhorrent to me.

You see, I'm inclined to go up and down on the scale of my emotions. To use another metaphor, it seems to me my life is a skein of many colored strands, black and white and all the colors in between, like the colors of the cloth that Fatima weaves. Yes, Fatima is a weaver and it is from her I get this metaphor. My emotional state moves from strand to strand in a colorful tapestry—sometimes in the white, sometimes in the red and blue and yellow, and sometimes in the black. I still don't understand what Baba means when he says, "Stay above good and bad, Mardana. They are the same." I only know that bad feels bad, and good feels good. And this time after smoking bhang, I fell into the bad, into the black. I tossed and turned all night, dark thoughts writhing in my brain like serpents.

Why hadn't God made me a nawab? I got to feeling discriminated against by life. I belonged to a lower caste; I was a servant; I didn't matter to the universe; others were so much better off than me. After a night of sleepless suffering, I finally fell asleep, but was soon woken by the clattering of pots and pans as the servants prepared the nawab's breakfast. When the sun came out the fat nawab emerged from his tent, and one servant shampooed his hair while the other massaged his feet. Later, he lay down on a cot in his underwear, and two servants massaged him while he chortled and groaned in pleasure. After that, he ate and drank huge quantities of food before the camp dismantled and the caravan took off again.

In my discontent, I grew angry at Baba. Nearly choking with anger and itching to get into a fight with him, I said in a tightly controlled voice, "Baba, is there one God for the rich and one for the poor? Those who worship the rich God get everything they want, but the poor have to scrape their knees raw, genuflecting on pebbles for a dried crust."

Baba looked at me, smiled, and said, "It would seem so, Mardana." I had expected some wise rebuke from him, and I was ready with my mental fists to knock down all his arguments and theories. But his ambiguous answer deflated me, though I was still mad and determined to have my fight.

"I thought you would say something about karma and our actions in the past life. I thought you would have an explanation, as you always do."

"I don't have an explanation, Mardana. What do I know? The divine design transcends human reasoning. High, low, rich, poor, good, bad—all of this is the Universe's inscrutable play. How can we know the mystery of inequality? We can only wonder and marvel at it. I only know that everything has a purpose, even though we cannot always see or guess at it. How can we, blind creatures, see the whole pattern of things? I only know that inner wealth far exceeds outer wealth in value, and that high or low, rich or poor, my Beloved beats in every heart."

"I'm done with your Beloved; I'm done with inner wealth. I'm not like you, Baba, I'm not a saint, but an undervalued artist with needs! I cannot live on God and Love and all those things you keep talking about," I continued. "You may be an enlightened being, but I am human, very human, and in need of all the things a human was made to need. How can I play this rabab and accompany you when you sing inspired songs, when even my fingers and vocal cords are weak? I am angry and crazed with hunger. Here, take your rabab. I am leaving you for good this time."

Baba took the rabab and was silent. I panicked. What would I do now? Where would I go?

"Even Kabir said to God, 'Here, take back your *mala*.[5] A hungry man cannot pray.'" I persisted.

"Kabir only asked God for essentials—flour, salt, beans."

"Ghee," I added. "He also asked for ghee. Times have changed, Baba. Everybody is asking God for more and more. I also have desires, and what's more, I like them. I like the many colors of maya. God is just an idea for the poor and disinherited to feel better. Fat nawabs and kings don't need God— they have everything they want. Just look at my shoes! Look at my rags! I would also like to wear silks, my bejeweled hand regally resting on my raised knee as I sit on my cushy, carpeted seat and survey my camp with a royal eye like a nawab. I don't want God, Baba, I want life, *life*."

"What makes you think you can't have God *and* life, Mardana?" Baba responded.

"Well, I haven't had any life so far. All I have had in your service is hunger and sore feet. Look at the nawab's servants. He gives them good food. He even gives them wine and bhang. I haven't told you," I said, ready to tear my relationship with Baba to bits, "but I . . . I love bhang. I crave it so much sometimes that I feel I can't breathe unless I have some."

"Ah, Mardana, what a wonderful thing you've said," Baba said, shutting his eyes, as he always does when he is deeply moved. I was very surprised at Baba's reaction. I wondered as I sat with him on the bank of the river what I had said that was so wonderful. Baba opened his eyes and said, "You show me how to love the Beloved, Mardana. You could love God like you love bhang, crave for God so much that you cannot breathe without Him. This longing is

---

[5] A string of beads serving as a rosary.

enough, the hunger is its own fulfillment. The longing is the union . . . " He let his sentence trail off.

I felt deflated. Baba had diffused all my rage, but I still felt cranky and dissatisfied. "But you have to eat sweet, rich food when you've taken bhang—halwa, *jaleibis, barfi, ladoos.*"[6]

We were sitting on the banks of the stream. Baba dug in the soft sand with his toe and picked up something.

"Take this to town," he said, putting something in my hand. "Sell it to whomever wants to buy it and use the money to buy a good meal."

It looked like just a stone to me—a pretty stone, but a stone. Parts of it were rough and occluded, and a small part of it was as translucent as a crystal.

"It's only a stone," I said.

"Mardana, open your eyes," Baba said.

I opened my eyes wide but I saw only a stone.

"Mardana, Mardana. When will you learn to see with the eyes of your heart?"

Baba is acting crazy again, I thought. *Who is going to give me a meal for this?*

But I decided to go to town with it anyway. I was so desperate for food and money that if no one bought it I was ready to sell one of my gems, regardless of the consequences. So I put on my robe, and off I went."

---

[6] Indian sweets.

CHAPTER 10

Gem

"The way to town was through gently rolling hills. All day I walked in what Baba calls the "pitch darkness of broad daylight," hungover, fearful, unhappy, twisted, and deformed inside. I was angry with the universe, with Baba, and with myself for smoking the bhang, which had destroyed my happiness and contentment. I felt full of self-hatred for being envious and greedy and always hungry for something or the other, knowing that contentment is possible, but unable to remove the thorn of envy from my heart. I walked, feeling that I would never be saved, that I should just crawl into a cave and die. Yet I kept moving toward the town, uncertain of my quest for food, thinking I was on a fool's errand. Who would pay me for this ordinary stone? And if I tried to sell one of my own gems, would I be robbed if people in the town found out about my treasure? Or would they think I had stolen it and take me to prison?

Suddenly it seemed to me that the stone in my pocket was humming or vibrating. I took it out, looked at it carefully, then put it to my ear, but there was no sound. I was about to put it back in my pocket, when it seemed to me a fire leaped out of it. Thinking that the bhang had unhinged my mind, I carried on.

But as I continued walking, I felt better. With the stone in my pocket, I walked over a few more hills into town. The bazaar had rows of well-stocked shops on either side of a narrow, cobbled street and was lively and full of *rawnak.*[1] Well-clad children played and shouted on the streets; handsome horses drummed their hooves on the cobbles as they pulled shining buggies carrying well-to-do citizens.

I went straight to a shopkeeper, showed him the stone, and asked what he would give me for it. He looked at it from all sides, and said, echoing my worst fears, "Nice stone; I'll give you a carrot for it."

A carrot! I thought, taking the stone back and walking to another shop. *I need something more than a carrot to appease my hunger.* I decided to try my luck at two more stores. The next shopkeeper merely glanced at the stone lying in the palm of my hand. "It's not worth anything, but my child could play with it. Here," he said, dangling a radish before my nose, "I'll give you this for the stone."

Fast losing hope, I went to another shop and repeated my offer. The shop-keeper held out his palm with a few peanuts in return for it. I was about to throw the stone at him when I noticed that someone was looking at the stone in my hand with a lot of curiosity. He looked like a beggar to me, unkempt, with a long beard and a conical, many-colored turban on his head. He looked at the stone with his fiery eyes and started to babble and mutter strange sounds, sort of like the sounds my crazy aunt, Daulatan Masi, the midwife who delivered Baba Nanak, makes. Even his eyes had the same strange intensity. Once the man stopped babbling, he fell into a trance and began to sway from side to side.

"He's crazy and dumb," the peanut seller told me. "He's a slave of Salis Rai, a very wealthy jeweler, famous throughout the world for his ability to recognize and appraise gems and who is always on the lookout for *the* gem. He employs this fool from the kindness of his heart and sends him into town to keep his eyes open for anything unusual."

"Maybe this pebble is the stone Salis Rai is looking for," another man said, provoking much laughter.

When the fool recovered from his trance, he bowed and scraped before me, then fell at my feet and kissed them. Stammering at first, then growing more coherent, he said, "Wah! Wah! Wah!"

Amazement silenced the peoples' laughter, and they gathered around him, all speaking at once. "Adhraka can speak! The fool can speak! He's not mute, after all! He was just pretending to be!"

---

[1] Hustling and bustling with life.

"Blessed! Blessed! Blessed!" said Adhraka, bowing before me.

People laughed at the spectacle of a fool calling an emaciated, ragged man selling a mere stone "Blessed!" and soon went back to their tasks as if nothing extraordinary had happened.

Adhraka gestured to me to follow him. I had nothing to lose, so I let him lead me through ever-narrowing gullies. He stopped in front of a door. Someone peeped through a slot, and it seemed to me they opened ten bolts and locks before opening the door and letting us in.

I had never seen so busy and cluttered a place as this. It was a jeweler's workshop, and men clad in loincloths were fanning fires with bellows; smelting metals in small and large crucibles above fiery furnaces; hammering gold on anvils; setting and annealing gems in rings, pendants, and bracelets; and chiseling, shaping, and faceting stones. We proceeded through the workshop to another room where the owner, Salis Rai, in a large turban and baggy pants, sat cross-legged on a fading red cushion, showing rings in small trays to two well-dressed and adorned silken ladies, who were poring over the tray with full attention, their ears and noses shimmering with diamonds. The fool waited patiently for his master to finish his business, while I looked around at the implements of the jeweler's trade—whetstones, scales, drills, and on the walls, small, carefully arranged glass bottles with beads and gems in them. The wall behind Salis Rai was full of tiny drawers, and over in one corner lay heaps of metal pieces and boxes full of rough and raw minerals.

Salis Rai was picking up gems with tiny tongs and weighing them on a miniscule scale whose weight measures were as thin as slivers of gold. Everything about his demeanor bespoke a man of intensity and passion. Here was a man who loved his stones and treasures, a man after my own heart. Watching him look at his gems with love and pride inflamed my own passion. My gems were so beautiful, so very beautiful. I longed to look at them again, touch them, and feel them the way Salis Rai was looking at his stones: with delight and pride of possession. As I stood there, I thought that if I could find some other way of being rich, I would keep my gems and every so often enjoy them far from the prying eyes of thieves. And off I went into a fantasy of how I would secure the gems in an underground room. I would bring them up one by one and look at them and touch them with the same passion that Salis Rai was displaying.

The ladies left, and Salis Rai looked up at me. He stared at me suspiciously with large eyes that I was certain had gotten that way from too much looking and searching. I knew he was wondering if I was a thief; I certainly wasn't dressed well enough for him to think I was a customer.

"What is it, Adhraka?" he said to the fool.

"Look, look!" Adhraka said to his master, who jerked his head up, amazed by his servant's newfound ability to speak.

"Adhraka! How is it you speak?"

The fool pointed at my palm with the stone in it. The jeweler looked at it lying in my palm and said, "Hmmm," then looked away and began to put his trays and bottles away.

He doesn't think it's anything, either, I thought, resolving to find a private place to pull out one of my own gems so I could at least buy a meal with it.

"Master! Master!" Adhraka persisted. "Look, look!"

This time the jeweler took the stone from my hand and squinted at it for a while. Then he put it on a shelf and resumed his previous activity.

"Well?" I asked, faint with hunger. "Are you going to buy it or not?"

"I have to test its worth, and that always takes time," he said.

"I don't have time!" I yelled. "Pay me something for it or I will die of starvation!"

The jeweler looked at me, and I realized how thin and pathetic I must look. He said to Adhraka, "Take him to the house and feed him, Adhraka. In the meantime, I will appraise this stone."

"*Hukum, hukum,*"[2] bowed the fool, and he took me to a house behind the shop where the jeweler's wife was cooking. She sat me down on the floor in the kitchen and placed a plate of *daal* and *rotis* before me. She even put a gob of ghee in the *daal*.

I ate well, though I didn't enjoy it as much as I could have on account of the thoughts going through my head about whether or not to sell some of my own jewels. *Perhaps,* I thought, *God sent me to an appraiser of gems for this purpose?* But the desire to show the appraiser my stones was attended by a host of fears. He would think I was a thief and have me arrested. Or he would overpower me—or perhaps even kill me—to possess the precious jewels.

---

[2] A very rich word in Sikh philosophy meaning "Divine Law," but in this instance meaning, "Your will, your will."

I returned to the shop, feeling much better with food in my belly. Salis Rai was looking at Baba's stone closely, intently. Old manuscripts were strewn around him. It seemed the more he looked at it, the more entranced he became with it.

"Adhraka," he said, giving the slave some money, "give him a tour of the town and come back in a few hours. Let him buy whatever he wants. I'm not done appraising the stone yet."

In town, the first place I stopped was a wine shop. I took the money from the slave and drank several glasses. Ah, the liquor in my belly changed the world and made it sparkle with life. Because I wasn't hungry and desperate, I was able to experience the sights and sounds of the town and enjoy myself thoroughly. I also enjoyed the way the fool treated me, with deference and respect, as if I were a nawab, as if I were rich despite my rags. He bowed before me and even dropped on the ground and kissed my feet! He kept saying, "Blessed! Blessed! Blessed!" But I knew not to get proud—after all, he was only a fool.

We returned to the shop once more. Salis Rai had an altered look on his face, as if he were in a trance. He held the stone in his hand, near his ear, and then near his heart. Then he opened his eyes and questioned me, "How did you get this stone? Who is your master? Tell me about him."

I told him about Baba and how he had unearthed the stone with his foot from the riverbed. After what seemed like a great deal of hesitation, Salis Rai reached into his pocket, brought out a gold coin, and gave it to me.

I was stunned, but I reached for it eagerly. A gold coin instead of a carrot! Baba and I would be taken care of for a while! I didn't need to risk selling any of my gems, though I was itching to rip them out and show the jeweler what I had. Putting the coin in my pocket and thanking Salis Rai, I was about to turn away when he said, "Take this with you."

He was holding Baba's stone in his hand. I hesitated, afraid he had changed his mind and wanted the money back.

"Keep the money," he said. "It is payment and thanks for giving me the privilege of a glimpse of your gem. Return it to your master. Tell him I can't afford to buy it. It is priceless."

I was confused, but also joyous. I had Baba's jewel and could sell it again when the need arose. Thrilled beyond measure to have a belly full of food, a gold coin, and a valuable gem in my pocket, I started back to camp. Salis Rai's servant, Adhraka, followed me. I tried to shoo him away, but he persisted. I supposed he wanted his commission, but I wasn't about to part with any of the money. I would have given him something if I had loose change, but I didn't have any. When nothing I did made him stop following, I ignored him. I supposed he would turn back when I walked out of town.

All the way back to camp I fantasized about our future. If the stone was indeed invaluable, we were set for the rest of the journey, maybe even the rest of our lives. I wouldn't have to sell the jewels in my hems after all. I would enjoy them, and when I died, I would bequeath them to my children. But oh, how the thought of dying and leaving the gems behind hurt my heart!

"Baba," I cried when I saw him sitting by the river, "Baba, you won't believe what happened." I rattled off my story, but Baba wasn't listening. His gaze was on something behind me. I turned around and saw that the fool had followed me all the way to the camp.

Adhraka ran to Baba and fell at his feet, kissing them and weeping, his whole body heaving with emotion. There was a wonderful smile on Baba's face as he lifted Adhraka up and clasped him to his heart and caressed his head.

I was very annoyed that Baba should clasp this dirty thing to his heart. I wanted to pry him away, but instead stood as a spectator, seething with anger and jealousy at the spectacle before me. They were laughing with each other in a friendly, playful way, like long-lost playfellows. There was such joy and love in them, such sweetness, that I felt left out, forlorn, an outsider. I knew that I would never know what it was to have Baba love me in such a way. As I stood and watched, an awareness of my own limited and depraved nature hit me like a wave of filthy water. I felt soiled in comparison. I couldn't think beyond money and food; I couldn't see or think beyond my eyes and material things. I was as shallow as water in a pan, blinded by my self; all I could see was my own puny reflection everywhere. I was so stuffed with thoughts of myself that they left room for nothing else. I hadn't even thought to bring Baba food!

Why would Baba bother to love me? I was deeply unlovable. I had disobeyed him; I had not practiced what we sang. Watching Adhraka braiding flowers in Baba's hair and feeling exiled from all the pure things of the world, I was about to flee when Baba said, "Come, Mardana, sit down and tell me what happened in town."

Feeling like a leper, I sat a little distance away from him and told him what had happened. I thought Baba would be pleased, but he said, "We will have to return the gold coin to Salis Rai. We cannot take something for nothing. Give the coin to Adhraka and he will take it back to his master." Adhraka looked very sad at the thought of returning to town, but he obeyed Baba instantly, bowing and saying, "Hukum, hukum." He took the coin, looked longingly at Baba, and left. I was annoyed with myself and wished I hadn't told Baba about the coin. However, I was happy to see the fool go.

"Baba," I blurted out. "You've never loved me the way you loved that fool! You never play with me like that!"

"That fool, Mardana, is my Beloved's fool. If you could see him with the eyes of your heart, you would have recognized that at once."

"Then help me see with the eyes of the heart. I have served you for so long, and what do I get in return?"

As soon as the words left my mouth I could see how foolish I was for saying such a thing. I was so twisted and anguished that I broke down and began sobbing.

"You are loved and lovable, Mardana," Baba said.

"Even though I am ugly, stupid, and without any virtue? Even though I am addicted to wine and drugs? Even though I am a fake, who sometimes pretends to feel the shabads he sings? Baba, you don't know me. I act as if I feel everything I play and sing, but I am very insincere in my love for God. I am full of lust, rage, greed, and pride—a bundle of all the vices in the world. There are many things I have done that I have never told you about, and I have many dirty little secrets. Even now, even now . . . " I wanted to blurt out about the gems in my hems, but some deep-seated and unshakable greed and lust for wealth kept me from confessing. I cleverly took the sentence in another direction and said, "Even now I feel dirty."

"How wonderful and wise, Mardana, that you admit this honestly! That you know what you are! Acknowledging your faults is the very first step toward becoming pure of heart!"

"But it's no consolation to me now, when I feel this ugliness oozing out of me," I replied.

"Give your ugliness and stupidity to the Pure One, Mardana. Turn to him, and he will embrace and love you, stupidity and all."

"But I don't deserve it! Tell me what I can do! Tell me just one thing I can do to evolve? I want to deserve your love!" I babbled. "Give me some specific instructions and I will try very hard to follow them faithfully, I promise!"

"Your own efforts will get you nowhere," Baba smiled. "You have to ask for help at every step. Make room in your heart for love, Mardana. Take one conscious step away from the entanglements of maya and one conscious step toward the Beloved."

"But I love maya! I love jewels and money and food, comforts and good clothes and shoes! I am not like you, Baba; I am just a human, in love with all aspects of this creation."

"And indeed, what a beautiful creation it is!" Baba said.

"I fear that in turning toward God I will have to give up all the things I love and long for!"

"Mardana, Mardana. God bestows life. In His service you only gain. There is a multiplication, not a subtraction. God gives more of life, more and more and more! You can also come to the Creator through the things you love. Continue to love them, Mardana. Go ahead, love creation, taste all the pleasures of life, for He is the giver of them. But remember the Creator: remember the Giver and keep him close. Clasp him to your heart!"

Baba was ecstatic. I knew bani was coming. I moved toward the rabab and began to strum it. It turned out to be one of those nights when we were both so attuned to each other that we were like two strings vibrating, flowing together into the Formless One's great, wide heart.

For a brief moment I saw another way of being—of giving myself entirely over to God, becoming His slave and letting him lead me wherever He wanted, of trusting Him as much as Baba trusted Him, with no restraints and fears, with just a sweet and total surrender. For a fleeting second I had a glimpse of being a slave of God, a pure soul, clasped to God's heart with chords of unending love. But the glimpse remained only a glimpse, like a point of light in the distance, a dream of perfection that tortured my heart when I compared it with my current, utterly human state. My mind was cut in two by these dualities, and despite Baba's reassurances that I could have more life if I surrendered to God, that I would be happier and more fulfilled, I continued down the cloven path, torn in two by my mind.

We were still singing when who came over the horizon on a horse but Salis Rai himself, accompanied by Adhraka and another servant. We discovered later that Salis Rai, deliberate and slow to react, had realized soon after I left that he wanted to meet the master of such a gem and had followed me. Salis Rai and his servants sat down quietly and listened to us sing, and when we were done, they laid two baskets before Baba and bowed low. The baskets were full of all sorts of delicious food, condiments, fruits, nuts, and sweets. Baba wouldn't eat till Adhraka had eaten, and Adhraka wouldn't eat till Baba had eaten; but once Adhraka realized Baba wanted him to eat first, he eagerly took a plate and ate with pleasure and joy. Then we all sat and ate heartily.

Later, in the fading light, Adhraka and I massaged Baba's feet, while Salis Rai bragged about what a good appraiser he was, telling incidents about his skill, about this and that gem, and this and that diamond. After a while, he came to the point.

"Guru Jee," Salis Rai said, "let me see your gem again!"

I took Baba's stone from my pocket and laid it in Salis Rai's palm. I could tell by the expression in his eyes that he coveted it—oh, how he coveted it!

Holding the stone gingerly in his hand, Salis Rai burst into praises of it.

"I have appraised many a gem in my life, but never have I seen anything like this. It is the gem I have been seeking all my life! From a certain angle it displays colors that have no name, that I have never, ever seen before! It needs to be cut, of course, for it is rough and raw, but from the clarity of just a fraction of it I can see what lies within! It is a mountain of light so luminous, so radiant, that the blind can see again, the mute speak! It is the lodestone that cures the sick, insane, crazy, and lost. My previously mute slave began to speak just by beholding it. I have found furrows running in the stone, inner lines of symmetry that are the edges of a crystal, indicating that this ordinary-looking stone consists of eight lines interpenetrating and projecting through each other. So rare and invaluable! The rarest of the rare! Extraordinarily brilliant! Perfect! Perfect! Ah, what a luminous being you are for owning it. Alas, I cannot afford it. Only the emperor—only the emperor dare consider it."

"It's not this stone that you are looking for, Salis Rai," Baba said, taking the stone from him and playfully tossing it in the air.

"Believe me, it is. There is no doubt. Don't underestimate my knowledge of gems."

"This is just a stone, a lovely, expensive stone, but just a stone," Baba said, as he tossed it in the air and let it fall into the river. All of us—except Adhraka, who laughed delightedly—let out a collective gasp of horror at Baba's action. Even in the fading light I could see that Salis Rai's face was ashen. He almost got up to dive in after it but knew, like the rest of us, that it was hopeless to try to find it again. He began to sputter in shock, and ultimately broke down and wept, repeating over and over, "To find it, only to lose it!"

"The stone was not what you were looking for, Salis Rai," Baba repeated. "For all your skill in appraising, you have been blind."

I could see that in addition to his horror at losing what he had just found, Salis Rai was offended that Baba should say such a thing to him.

"Me, blind? I have the best eye in the whole world when it comes to gems!"

"Then how do you not know that you already have the gem you are looking for?"

Salis Rai looked befuddled, as if groping in the darkness for some meaning to Baba's words. I could see he was struggling, as all of us were, to understand.

"You're wrong," he said after a while. "I don't have it. I have carefully cataloged all my gems and inspected them hundreds of times. I have graded them and kept aside a handful of the rarest of them all."

"This gem you are looking for is not a thing," Baba smiled.

Salis Rai sat quietly for a long time, his brow wrinkled in deep thought, the powers of his brain concentrated as if deciphering a puzzle. After a long time, a light gleamed in his eye, and he said, "Is it you, Guru Jee? Are you the gem I am looking for? Is it your wisdom that you mean? I can see that there is a glow in your eye that shines like the brightest of diamonds. Yes, I think it is you."

"The crystalline lens of the awakened consciousness that we attain when we surrender to the Limitless One is the gem. It is richer than all the treasures of the world put together, Salis Rai, and it can never be lost. When we see through it, all matter, all forms, all life, and all nature are luminous and undying. Seek it, Salis Rai, seek what you already have but must find all over again. Seek it with an open mind and heart. And when you find it, treasure it above all else. Cut it, Salis Rai, and remove the encrustations upon it; polish it and keep it clean, and you will be the wealthiest man in the whole world."

Baba's words rang out sweetly and clearly under the sapphire sky, now filling up with bright shining stars. We all sat silently for a long time.

"But how do I seek it? Where shall I begin?" Salis Rai asked.

Baba quoted a line from his bani: "Aap veechaarai so parkhay heeraa." (One who contemplates his own self tests the worth of the jewel.)

Salis Rai fell at Baba's feet and said, "You, you are the gem. I never want to part with you again. Come home with me and I will provide you a house with all the conveniences you require."

Of course Baba refused, and Salis Rai was more distraught at the thought of never seeing Baba again than he had been over the loss of the stone. He wept and pleaded. It looked as if Adhraka was about to join his master in his supplication to Baba to stay, but he didn't. He stood quietly with hands folded, ready to obey Baba's word, whatever it might be.

"You don't need me when you have another gem with you. It has been before your eyes all the time, and you, unaware, have not appraised it, Salis Rai."

Baba put his arm around Adhraka's shoulders and said, "This is your real gem. You have him instead of me."

Adhraka did not refute Baba, but just stood calmly by. Salis Rai looked at Baba, then Adhraka, then at Baba again, who nodded.

Salis Rai fell at his slave's feet and I did the same, utterly ashamed of myself for having been so very blind. Adhraka shone like a bright star, and now that Baba had opened my eyes I could see beyond his appearance to the light that he was. Adhraka quietly lifted us up and embraced each one of us to his heart.

"I will be your slave henceforth," Salis Rai said to Adhraka. "Command and I will obey. Like you, I will say, 'Hukum, hukum.'"

"No, please don't take away from me my need to serve. Service is my only pleasure, my true joy. Let me serve you, master, for by serving I have learned whatever little I know; serving has made me what I am."

Sitting in the starlight that night, Baba sang many a shabad. The one I recall most clearly is:

Alga-o jo-ay madhookarha-o sarangpaan sabaa-ay,
heerai heeraa baydhi-aa naanak kanth subhaa-ay.
(One who is unattached like the bumblebee, sees the Beloved everywhere.
The diamond of his heart is pierced through with the
diamond of His name.
O Nanak, his neck is embellished with it.)

Adhraka and Salis Rai stayed through the night and in the morning prepared to leave. Salis Rai wept again and kept looking back at Baba as he moved away. But Adhraka moved strongly ahead, a spring in his gait, his robe flowing and swishing about his ankles."

⸺

Mardana paused in his story. Tears were flowing down his muzzle. "I am the blind one. I am the fool, the real fool. Why, oh why does it take a final separation to see what something was and is? Why was I so blind to Baba's light?"

CHAPTER 11

From the Roof
of the Fish's Belly

The next morning before dawn, one enchantress came into the pen and took two of the goats away. This was always a difficult moment for the other goats, as it reminded them of their imminent death. They mourned the loss of their companions, but also rejoiced that it wasn't them.

Mardana slept late, as usual. He had been unwilling to awaken and face the day till Mannay nudged him with his horns.

"I slept well last night after hearing your stories and was reassured that such a man as Nanak lives. If one man can transcend human greed and fear, it gives me hope about the universe and my place in it," Mannay said. "Perhaps in a small way I could still become a better human being."

"Bahhh . . . a better goat, you mean," Taakat said, incorrigible despite his wounds. "We are as much locked into our natures as goats are. We have no control over our destinies."

"Baba says that, too," Mardana said, yawning. "That we are what our destiny intends us to be."

"So what's the point of this spiritual struggle then?" Taakat said. "What's the point of making an effort to change?"

"Effort is essential, Baba says. By *effort* he means a subtle gesture, an inner turning toward the True One. Baba has a name for this act, for the person who turns toward God—*gurmukh*, meaning someone whose face is turned toward the Guru, as opposed to a *manmukh*, someone whose face is turned toward his own willful mind and ego. I have always been a manmukh. My own desires have always mattered to me most.

"So finally, Rondoo, let me tell you what happened to the treasure."

The goats on the other stakes, who had heard the stories in bits and pieces, craned their necks to hear.

"THROUGHOUT ALL OF OUR TRAVELS, I succeeded in hanging on to my treasure. Baba wanted to go south, to Sri Lanka, while I wanted to go north, to Sultanpur, to secure my jewels. I had arrived at a point where the importance of my treasure far exceeded my attachment to Baba. All I wanted to do was get home, sell my jewels, settle down, and never, ever leave home again. I wanted to have my own life and live according to my own desires. Besides, my knees, hips, and back were all aching, and all I wanted was a nice clean bed to sleep in for a hundred years. But Baba loved to wander from place to place, country to country, across the seas and over the mountains. Though he reassured me our journeys were coming to an end, that we only had one or two more adventures left, I didn't believe or trust him.

We reached the very southern tip of India, from where we were going to board a ship for Sri Lanka. I pretended to be sick. I limped exaggeratedly, clutched my chest, and rolled my eyes, but Baba ignored me. I kept looking for opportunities to escape from him. Twice I tried to get lost in the crowds that were boarding the many ships in the harbor, but Baba knew what I was thinking and stayed close to me, his smiling eyes looking through my soul. I now know it was because he wanted to save me from the harvest of my rebellion.

We boarded the ship with the others, jostling on the gangplank, everyone with their bundles and loads, some very well dressed, but most, like us, in shabby clothes. We settled in a corner of the deck, poor pilgrims that we were. I was cold, but the thought of my loaded hems kept me warm and happy. High-class people with luggage and wearing expensive clothes went to their fancy cabins. I chuckled to myself, thinking about how they didn't know that I was actually wealthier than they were. Next time we traveled—but no, there was not going to be a next time. This was absolutely my last journey. I would reach home and never leave.

We lifted anchor and off we went. At night, dark clouds gathered and moved quickly, obscuring the full moon and then revealing it for a few brief moments before covering it again. A terrible storm arose, with fiendish winds that tossed our ship from the crests of high waves to abysses that seemed to swallow us up. I was terrified at the boat's violent rolling and pitching, but Baba wanted me to play the rabab, of all things! All of the frightened people on deck and some from their cabins came to listen to us in an effort to calm their terror. My fingers trembled upon the strings, but when thunder and lightning revealed Baba's face momentarily, he was calm, serene, and radiant, despite the impending danger. His eyes shut, he sang:

> Jap tap ka bandh bairula jit langai vahaila
> na sarvar naan oochalai aisa panth suhaila.
> (Embark on the raft of meditation and self-discipline,
> and there will be no ocean, no fierce storm or raging waves;
> your path will always be easy and pleasant.)

But I didn't hear a word—no, not a word—for I was afraid of losing my life and my treasure. I can say now that my ego had plugged up my ears. I was like a deaf man listening only to the cacophony inside his own head while all around him angels sang. I had visions of being tossed into the water and drowning, of lying dead at the bottom of the ocean with fishes nibbling on my nose, my ears, and my gems.

I wondered whether it was my disobedience to Baba's command to get rid of the gems that had caused this storm. After much vacillation, I finally realized the value of my life was so much greater than the value of my gems, so I took my cloak and flung it into the water."

———

"Oh!" gasped the goats. "After all that trouble!"

———

"AND BEHOLD, THE STORM CEASED almost instantaneously! At once I thought, looking at the calm waters rippling in the moonlight, *Fool! Fool! You threw your treasure overboard for nothing!*

I spent several hours beating my head against the railing. When I looked down at the water again, what did I see but my robe floating alongside the boat in the calm sea! *God wants to return my treasure to me!*

In the distance I could see the lights of a town glimmering in the night air. We were near shore, and I decided to risk it. I would dive into the water, escape Nanak, retrieve my garment and my treasure, then swim to shore. The water looked calm, and I was a strong swimmer, having practiced swimming upstream in the Beini River on warm summer days with Baba for the sheer fun and challenge of it. I decided to take my rabab along with me. If the sea became rough again, I could ride its buoyant body. When I got to town I would sell a gem and buy my way back home—first class, of course.

It sounded like an excellent plan to me. So while Baba slept, I jumped, rabab in hand, from the deck into the sea. Buoyed up by the rabab, I half floated and half swam toward my robe, which bobbed up and down in the calm sea, just barely out of reach. A beneficent current carried me toward it, and I felt certain in my heart that it was God's sweet will to rescue me, treasure and all, so I could lead the life I deserved. But every time I almost grasped the fabric, a current took the robe away from my fingertips. A thousand times I almost had it, and a thousand times it bobbed right out of my reach. Finally, O heaven, I had it in my grasp!"

The goats heaved a collective sigh of relief.

"When I looked around I saw that in attempting to retrieve my treasure, I had drifted away from the boat *and* the shore. In a very short time, things went from being very right to very wrong, and I began to panic. Shivering and trembling in the waters, I sensed the presence of strange sea creatures circling beneath and all around me. The movement became stronger, faster, and suddenly, with a deafening splash, a huge fish, its scales shimmering blindingly bright in the moonlight, leaped out of the water, and its gigantic jaws, full of saberlike ivory teeth, gaped wide like Hell's gate and swallowed me whole—robe, rabab, and all."

Mardana paused to regain his breath. The description of the fish conjured up his experience all over again, and his heart was palpitating within his furred breast. The lower jaws of his audience dropped, as they gaped at him in awe and disbelief.

"EVERYTHING WAS SILENT. I WASN'T dead. I looked around and found myself in the fish's mouth, light filtering in through its teeth like rays through prison bars. I was calm and alert, with just one thought in my mind: I was going to survive this with my cleverness and strength. I would defeat this beast; I would kill it. The stand of my rabab had a pointed prong on it, and I was planning to gash the fish from the inside and fight my way out. But as I stood there, a low sound reverberated all around me. It sounded to my human ears like "Surrender!"

"Never!" I shouted. Standing on the fish's tongue, I twanged my rabab in bravado, but its strings sounded limp and damp. I sang loudly, but my voice, too, gurgled and spluttered. A movement of the fish toppled me to the floor of its slimy tongue. I use the word *floor* because yes, fellow goats, its mouth was as big as a large room, with a throbbing gullet at the end of it—an end that I was fast approaching. Determined not to die, I rammed my rabab lengthwise in its throat trying to stop my descent, but it was a futile attempt, for I slipped easily through the passage with several yards to spare on either end.

Again I heard the word "Surrender!" thundering deep and low all around and within me. As I said "Never!" I slithered on my belly through a long tube that vibrated and pulsed, while acrid, acidic juices from the monster's digestive tract splashed on my clothes and burned my skin. Despite this, I was still alert, still awake, and determined to live. I began to jab the forked metal stand of the rabab into the walls of the fish's liver, stomach, and intestines, but its insides were made of such a jellylike material that the edges of the gashes came together and healed right before my eyes. I had never seen anything like it before. I began to panic when I realized this thing might be immortal. The tube I was traveling in became narrower and narrower, squeezing me in its pulsations, and just as I thought I was going to pass out, I was delivered to a large red chamber with dim light filtering in through the beast's scaly skin. Once again I felt powerful and more than capable of overcoming this ordeal, sure that I could kill the fish in the process. A marvelous fragrance like nothing I have ever smelled before permeated the room. Feeling hungry, I reached out, grabbed some of the material the wall was made of, and ate it. I had never tasted anything like it before. It filled me with energy and power. I looked around and saw the remains of many fish that the beast had eaten, half chewed and dismembered. My jewels, too, lay scattered in the fish's entrails among other treasures the fish had swallowed from wrecked ships—gold coins, jewelry, ornaments, and implements, to name a few. The beast had also eaten a fishing line, in which I soon became hopelessly entangled. The more I tried to extricate myself from the tangle, the more the line tightened around me. The walls of the room, too, squeezed together and started to churn violently, almost suffocating me. I was smothered in the bloody remains of other fish, their bones puncturing my skin. I cried out in pain and fear as I tumbled in the beast's belly. All the tumult around me seemed again to be saying, "Surrender! Surrender!"

Fellow goats, I cannot describe to you in words what happened next. I can only use feeble, inadequate images, none of which will fully explain or describe my experience. I have been telling you stories with plots in which things happened, this and then that and that. But nothing *happened* in the belly of the fish—only some inner experience that will sound vague to you. But let me try to give you an idea.

First of all, I was afraid, as you can imagine. I knew that this thing was so powerful that there was no way I was going to survive it. I knew in the marrow of my bones that I was going to die. My whole life flashed before me: scenes from my childhood, Baba's birth, my experience with the rabab, my marriage to Fatima, my dog Moti, all my travels, all the stories I have told you, and so much, much more. This was not just a remembering, you understand. It was presence, *reliving*, in every detail. And all of this happened in one minute of our time. Recalling it later, I realized that our past is preserved in some loop and gyre of time. Our past is not destroyed, as we think, and our present time is not the only time there is. There is a space right within our time that is spaceless and timeless. But, let me stay with the story. Death stared me in the face and suddenly in my mind's eye played the scene in the *modikhana* in Sultanpur: Baba, his eyes half shut in a trance, shoveling grain and lentils into the spread skirts, shirts, and turbans of the beggars and the poor, and repeating over and over, "Tairra, tairra, tairra."

Tairra, tairra, tairra echoed in my skull and in the belly of the fish, bouncing off its walls. I knew in that moment, as I churned and tumbled, that nothing, nothing at all, not even my body and breath—let alone my treasure—belonged to me. And in an inner gesture of assent, I surrendered all that I thought was me and mine to that which had birthed me from nothing and was about to return me to that nothing again. *This, too, is yours. Tairra, tairra, tairra.*

I felt myself being cut up and dismembered, ground down to meat and bones. And then, fellow goats, I died."

———— ⋅◦✦◦⋅ ————

Mardana paused, expecting the goats to object, but by now they were used to Mardana's fantastic stories, sensing the inner, metaphoric logic to them. They remained silent, happy to be entertained and instructed, knowing Mardana would answer their questions in due time. Mardana was heartened by this and carried on with the thread of his story.

"I know I died," Mardana resumed, "because my spirit rose above my body, hovered on the roof of the fish's belly, and saw the scene below. I felt like someone else watching Mardana's dismembered body entangled like a fish in a net, pulsing in the peristalsis of digestion, his precious gems strewn here and there amidst the hooks, nets, and remains of other dead sea creatures. I saw it as if from a star, with total and utter detachment, unmoved by the drama beneath me. I was *in* the Sea of God's Great Heart and all my troubles, my losses, my life, and my death were holy, holy, holy. I felt like a particle of light, weightless, with feelings that I can only describe with inadequate words like released, free, happy, and blissful. Nothing—not the walls of the fish's skin, not the shell of my body, not the cage of my skull, not my life, my wife, my children, my attachments, dreams, or desires—could contain or constrain me. I turned and followed the light-filled, joyous path to whatever unbounded ecstasy lay ahead, excited to begin the celestial journey toward my home in my maker's heart."

Mardana was silent a long time. The goats knew not to disturb him in his memory of that moment. In the stillness, they too felt the stirring of hope in their hearts that whatever lay ahead was good and sweet, beyond and above what their minds could imagine or conceive.

"Yes, I died," Mardana resumed after a while. "Baba Nanak has always said, 'Die before you die, and then there shall be no death. Die into the Beloved, and you will live forever.'"

Mardana paused. A glimmer of light flashed in his brain, and he felt the dawn of a deep understanding. His heart dilated with gratitude that he had been given the task and gift of storytelling, which had shown him the way to make his final days a sacrament and a surrender. The light bloomed in his mind, and he realized that by telling and remembering the stories, he had not only enlightened his fellow goats, but had been enlightened himself. Mardana felt regret rising in his breast that his thick skull had not understood sooner, but his newly acquired understanding pushed the emotion aside. There was no time for regret; his days must be informed with gratitude.

Mardana shut his eyes again, as if tasting some *atam ras*, or soul nectar. He was a little annoyed when Rondoo nudged him with his horns to continue his story, but with his annoyance came the thought that he must not leave his audience hanging; that he must continue, not only because of them, but also because he himself had many lessons to learn. Mardana continued his story.

⇒⊶●⊷⇐

"I OPENED MY EYES AND saw that I was still inside the fish, in a chamber resembling a large balloon. I knew that I was in the fish's womb. Yes, the fish was female, and she, emissary of God, was about to birth me. Her breathing became labored, and soon I was disgorged, rabab and all, in a swish and slosh of waters on the shores of the sea.

Celestial music poured into my newly birthed ears like *amrit*, the ambrosia of the gods. It was as though I had been birthed into a new world. Dewdrops were glistening on the emerald palm trees like diamonds in all their fiery colors; the sun was pouring its sweet, warm, golden light on me, and I was in total bliss, with not a thought or question in my head.

When I eventually turned toward the source of the music, there was Baba, sitting on the sands with a few others, singing. The sight of Baba, the sound of his bani, the touch of the sun upon my skin, warm and sweet like honey, and the smell of the sweet air caressing me like a mother were heaven. I was alive, newly birthed from the womb of death, and listening to Baba's precious, precious voice, as he sang the Song of the Fish."

Too daree-aa-o daanaa beenaa mai machhulee kaisay ant lahaa.
Jah jah daykhaa tah tah too hai tujh tay niksee foot maraa.
(You are the immeasurable ocean
How can I, a fish, know your limits?
Wherever I look
You are there.
Separated from you
I burst and die.)

CHAPTER 12
Rondoo's Sacrifice

The inevitable happened. One night, as rain from the broken roof was pelting down into the soggy pen, two enchantresses carrying the can of indelible red paint came into the pen and painted Rondoo's forehead.

Though they had all known this could happen any day to any one of them, the goats were shocked that one from their own group had received the red mark. Rondoo had only one night before he would be taken and slaughtered. This fact brought the reality of death home to all of them.

"No!" Rondoo screamed the single word again and again after he had recovered from his speechless shock. "No, no, no, no, no! I don't want to die. I'm not ready. I haven't lived yet! This can't happen to me! I won't let it. I'll . . . I'll kill them; I'll gore them with my horns; I'll run away; I'll do something; I'll . . . "

When his rage subsided, Rondoo went into a corner and became very morose. Mardana, who had grown rather fond of him, was also very sad and upset. He walked over to Rondoo's corner and nudged him gently. Rondoo looked at him and burst into tears.

"What is life all about?" he wept. "I've had a miserable life—a wife who treated me like dirt, parents who thought me a failure, a society that treated me like excrement because I am an untouchable—all experiences that delivered me to goathood in a pen. And now I must die!"

"At least you'll be released from your miserable life," Mardana consoled, but this only made Rondoo weep all the more.

"Life is meaningless! You suffer and then you die!"

"Suffering," Mardana said, "is never useless, especially when you suffer with courage. Know that reincarnation is real, and those who suffer well here get their rewards in the next life."

Mardana wondered if he truly believed this. In any case, believing certainly lessened one's anxiety.

"I don't want some next life. Can't you summon your Baba to save me, like he saved you so many times?" Rondoo pleaded.

"Let us take God's name," Mardana said, "for that was what saved me from the cannibals."

"That was just a story!" Rondoo despaired. "This is real! Do you think I can get out of this by simply reciting God's name?"

"No," said Mardana. "No one has ever escaped from here."

"Then what's the use? What's the stupid use?"

"It will calm you down; it will give you peace."

"I don't want peace and calm! I want life! More life!"

"We all have to die, Rondoo—some sooner than others."

"Why do I have to go sooner? Why is it always me that has to go sooner?"

"Shall I sing for you? Shall I tell you another story?"

"No! I don't want to waste the little time I have listening to stupid songs and stories!"

Rondoo was agitated beyond words, and Mardana didn't know what to say. Mardana stayed quiet, for what can one truly say in the face of such suffering? He decided to simply be present and patient.

Mardana listened as Rondoo told him all about his miserable life. Rondoo was in the throes of mortal suffering, and Mardana was wise enough to know that his agitation must take its course before any wisdom could step in and help. So he just sat by Rondoo and let him bleat and moan, scream and rage.

As he listened, Mardana marveled at how unreal death is to all of us till the very moment it is upon us; he mused about how little prepared we are for it, even though we know all along that this will be our inevitable end. *I'm wiser than Rondoo*, Mardana thought.

When Rondoo quieted down a bit, Mardana began to hum to himself. Rondoo once again broke down at the sound.

"I will never hear you sing again! I will never hear another story again!"

"At least you got to hear the end of the story of the treasure," Mardana reassured him.

"It didn't end well!"

"Listen carefully, Rondoo," Mardana said, with the weight of his recently acquired wisdom. "Everything in life, including me and you, is a sacrifice."

"To this evil woman? If I were being sacrificed to a god or goddess, it might be worth it. But to spill my blood so the bitch can bathe in it and eat my warm, still-palpitating heart? What kind of sacrifice is that?"

"The truth is far bigger than you think, Rondoo. No matter what causes our death, *our death is always a sacrifice*—don't you see?"

"No, I don't. It's just something you are making up to make me feel better."

"Look at it this way. You are dying so that the rest of us can have a few more days of life. You are dying for us."

"I wish you were dying for me instead," Rondoo said.

"Okay, think of it like this. You have had a life because so many others have died. Everything before you has sacrificed itself for you."

"Who? What?"

"Your father. Your mother. All your ancestors died so you may live. The other goats died so you could live a few more days."

"I still don't understand. Add stupidity to the long list of my faults."

"Okay, let's simplify it. The hay you have been eating has sacrificed itself, died, so you could eat it and have energy for life."

"I don't think it is the same thing. Grasses don't have our kind of life."

"Baba says everything, including inanimate nature, is alive."

"It's not the same thing. Grasses don't bleed."

"Okay, fine. I will say it." Mardana said reluctantly. "Have you ever eaten a goat?"

"Yes."

"Why?"

"Because it tasted good . . . "

"And because it gave you the energy for life?"

"Yes."

"Well, there you are."

It took a second for Rondoo to catch on, and then he let out such a wailing that all the other goats in the pen woke up and swore at Rondoo and told him to shut up. They had heard these cries many times before and had made a pact, frequently broken, that goats should spend their last nights in silence so as not to disturb the others.

"Hush, hush," Mardana said. "Be consoled. Know that each part of you will be utilized."

But this only agitated Rondoo more. Mardana realized that he could not help the doomed goat, so he returned to his corner and lay down. *One can sacrifice only so much of one's sleep for another*, he thought. He was so tired he fell asleep almost immediately.

Mardana awoke to Rondoo nudging him with his horns.

"I want to tell you something," he said. Mardana saw that Rondoo looked sad, but calm.

"After you fell asleep I felt dreadful, but I remembered something you said earlier about surrendering to suffering, embracing instead of resisting it. I surrendered my darkness to Nanak. I said, 'If you can love low castes like Adhraka, then love me a little, too. If you say your God forgives the dumbest and stupidest, then perhaps He could forgive me, too. Give me a sign that I am forgiven and loved.' But there was no sign, and I despaired. Then suddenly the rain stopped, and some light, like the visitation of an angel, came into the pen, softly and gently. It was the moon, shining down on me from that crack in the roof. It felt like a sign! I felt very blessed to be able to see the moon. I knew I was loved! I knew I mattered! I thought of myself as a sacrifice for others, and I felt my life had meaning, and it calmed me down. Thank you. I will carry this feeling in my heart all the way to the altar."

Footsteps outside the pen heralded that the moment had come. The enchantresses were here to take Rondoo away. Rondoo looked at Mardana fearfully, but Mardana's eyes met his reassuringly and he calmed down.

"Yes, and I did hear the end of the story," Rondoo said. The women seemed distracted as they guided him out, and they did not kick Rondoo or yank at his tether.

"Remember," Rondoo said to the other goats, who were now standing alert to bid him good-bye, "I am dying today so you may have more time to live.

Keep me present in your hearts!"

Rondoo was happy to see tears in the eyes of his friends and to know he would be missed and present in their memories. Then he turned around and let himself be led away.

A gloom fell upon the pen. Rondoo's fellow goats were very sad. Even Taakat, it seemed, was pensive and thoughtful. This death was too close for them to deny their own impending demise.

CHAPTER 13
The Red Mark

The night before the full moon, the sorceresses marked all of the goats in Mardana's pen for sacrifice to Nur Shah.

Sidda bleated pitifully while the rest of them stood quietly, their heads hanging down. It was not a moment for words or storytelling, but for each to be alone with his fears and feelings. This was the end of the road for each, the moment for which they were born, the inevitable goal of their lives. Death is always too far away until it is too near.

Time dilated with Mardana's awareness of each passing second, and his feelings took many a turn and twist before morning came.

Mardana's wisdom and faith, always precarious when compared with Baba's unshakable anchoring in God, crumbled all about him. He was just a naked creature face-to-face with his end. He felt like an ant about to be squashed.

Mardana recalled an incident long ago. Outside Saiyidpur, which Emperor Babar had sacked, slaughtering its inhabitants mercilessly, Baba Nanak and he had happened upon an area filled with the corpses of women, children, and young men.

"If there is a God, why does He allow such things to happen, Baba? Why did Babar kill so many?" Mardana had asked. "Granted, a few Pathans[1]

---
[1] A tribe from Afghanistan and northern Pakistan, also called Pashtuns. The men tend to be warriors.

had offended the emperor, but why kill everyone? Why do tyrants kill the innocent along with the guilty? If I were God, I would have made a better, less violent world."

It was a hot, sultry night, and they were sitting under the stars. Baba had said, "We will discuss it in the morning," but Mardana was so agitated he couldn't sleep. Baba touched him on the head and said, "Sleep, Mardana."

Mardana had lain under a tree, and as he slept, a few drops of honey from a hive above him fell on his chest. He woke to ants crawling all over his body, and he squashed them all, rubbing them hard with the palm of his hand.

"Ants!" Mardana thought. "We are just ants to God, like people were ants to Babar!"

Mardana realized that his words of wisdom to Rondoo were just hot air. He felt he had been a fool for believing in Providence; he wasn't any wiser than when he had started out on the journey. Taakat, who was sitting quietly, going through his own death journey and looking like a crumpled bundle of dirty black fur, had been right all along, Mardana thought. He, Mardana, would go to his death like Taakat, knowing he had ripped through the illusion of God to the truth of things, and the truth was nothing, nothing, nothing!

Mardana had always wanted to die in good spirits. "God," he had prayed repeatedly, "when it is my time to die, please let me come to you joyously." He wished he had some wine or bhang to deaden his pain and alleviate his suffering and was saddened and angry at his ignominious death. He would crawl on all fours to some dark goddess's altar to have his head chopped off, left to roll about on the ground and bleed.

The thought caused such a severe pain in his neck and such a loud cacophony in his head that he broke the rule and bleated raucously. He felt he was being roasted alive in fire. He recalled an image from one of Baba's songs:

> Jee-arhaa agan baraabar tapai bheetar vagai kaatee.
> (My heart is on fire and a blade is slicing through it.)

When the bleating and screaming didn't help, he burst into a paroxysm of prayer.

"Please, God, Baba, Friend . . . I know I am a stupid, useless, insincere, egotistical manmukh, but if I have sung even one shabad, even just one line of one shabad, or even just one note of one shabad with sincerity and love for you, give me your hand and save me from this fiery ocean in which I am about to drown. Help this sinking stone swim, Supreme One!"

In the calm that followed his outburst, the second line of Baba's song came to him:

Paranvat naanak hukam pachhaanai sukh hovai din raatee.
(Help me to recognize Your Will, and be at peace night and day.)

In that instant Mardana knew that his being was so entangled with God that it was as impossible to live without Him as for a fish to live without water. He heard Baba's voice in his head say, *"Sleep, Mardana."* How often had Baba said these words to him while his unending and troubled thoughts made him toss and turn as they slept on the ground in their many travels? Every time, whether in a forest, field, or valley, or on a mountain, or at the seashore, his thoughts would be lulled to rest and he would drift off into blessed sleep.

The imagined words had the same effect, and Mardana slept. He dreamed that all this business of being a goat was just a nightmare and that he was reunited with Baba Nanak, who said to him, "Mardanaia, bani aee hai, rabab chhaid." He picked up the rabab, and after the first few strains of the song, he awoke. But the song stayed with him, and in a passionate voice he began to sing:

Saajan days vidaysee-arhay saanayhrhay daydee.
Saar samaalay tin sajnaa mundh nain bharaydee.
(O Friend, you who are so far away, I send you my message of love!
I remember you, my Friend, with tears.
I am lost on this treacherous path.
How can I cross over and find you, my Beloved, my Lord?)

It was a sincere cry, and his soul reached out with arms of longing to the Beloved. The other goats awoke and listened and found the song resonating in their own hearts. Their feelings, tangled in their heads as they faced their impending doom, descended into their hearts, and they, too, wept.

The remaining time, at the other goats' request, was spent in Mardana singing many of Baba Nanak's shabads.

Sarfai sarfai sadaa sadaa ayvai ga-ee vihaa-ay.
Naanak kis no aakhee-ai vin puchhi-aa hee lai jaa-ay.
(Bit by bit, life passes away, even though the mortal tries to hold it back.
O Nanak, unto whom should we complain?
Death takes one's life away without anyone's consent.)

CHAPTER 14
The Glowing Eyes of Death

When Mardana had finished singing, the door of the pen opened, and Razaa and her friends came in to fetch the goats for the sacrifice. The day, though not yet the moment, of their death had arrived. Mardana found he was anything but resigned to his fate. As Razaa untied him from the stake, he dug his heels into the dirt and gave her a kick or two before sitting down defiantly. She returned the favor with her stick, with which she was not gentle. He was quickly forced off his rump and led outside.

Mardana was stunned by the beauty of the moment, at the very cusp of night and day, when it is neither and both. It was what Baba Nanak called *amrit vela*, the ambrosial hour, the best time of the day to connect with God through meditation, chanting, and song. The orb of the full moon glowed like a pearl against the steel blue sky of early morning. The crisp, cool, mysterious breeze called *malyanil*, the breeze that brings intimations of eternity, was blowing gently. Mardana marveled at the magic of the morning. Though he had been up at this hour many times in his journeys with Baba, it was as if he were seeing the beauty that was always there for the very first time. His ears heard the liquid, lyrical notes of birdsong and the thought struck him: *I have gone from here to there and done this and that, thought, and felt, and experienced, but not as someone who lived with the consciousness of death. How lovely this earthly paradise is! We are here for one purpose only: to admire, praise, and love God's handiwork. I have never seen the wealth that is life! Baba saw life like this all the time—Baba, who is a liberated being, and who sees life through the fiery, glowing eyes of death.*

Mardana thought about how courageous and fearless Baba Nanak was before every encounter with death, while he himself had whimpered and wept like a coward; like a Marjana.

I could have had untold spiritual wealth, and I squandered it away for a mere shell. Oh give me another chance at life, God, please!

But what does it mean to live, to be alive? An unequivocal answer came to Mardana: *When I sang with Baba and his words touched my heartstrings and the music vibrated throughout my entire being, I was pulsating with life.*

A shadow fell across Mardana, but he was so full of regret that he didn't notice it. A sudden movement behind him made Mardana turn around. Mannay had dropped to the ground on his knees, his head bowed before someone clad in a cloak.

Mardana squinted at the human form, not believing his eyes.

"So, Mardana, the day has arrived," Baba said. Mardana was certain he was hallucinating, but Baba looked and sounded very real. Was his mind playing tricks with him?

"You should have taken my advice and given your head to the Beloved, friend. Now you're going to have to give it to Maya."

"My Baba! My Baba has come! This is my Baba, the one that I have been talking about! He has come to save us all!" Mardana bleated excitedly.

"I can do nothing, Mardana," Baba said.

"Help us, help us! Save us! We're all going to die!" they bleated.

Baba, who understood their bleating, said, "It is not up to me, but take comfort in the fact that you will be fitting sacrifices to the goddess. What fat, handsome goats you are! No part of you will be wasted. Drums and rugs will be made of your fur and skin; I'll buy the rug they make with your fleece, Mardana. I have always wanted one to meditate on. Your gut will become strings for musical instruments, your skin parchment for poets like me to write on."

"Stop, Baba, stop!"

"And though in the raw you will be a little frightening—food for philosophy and ruminations—roasted in the fire and cooked, you will be delicious. Perhaps they will give me a little bit of you to eat, Mardana. Which part of you should I request?" Guru Nanak said jovially.

"My brain, Baba, my stupid, ignorant, blind brain!" Mardana wailed. "But if you save me, I will give my head to God, I promise! I will wake up early and sing with you! Please, just save me!"

"The summons has come. It is here; it is now."

"I will accept it, Baba; I will have to when it comes, but does it have to be now? I want to survive, to see my children and grandchildren, my dog Moti, and of course, Fatima! I just want to put my head in her lap and weep, feel the skin of her hand on my hair and on my face. Please have mercy on me."

"Mardana, instead of bleating and crying, remember the Timeless One. Remember, and you'll have a peaceful death and hereafter."

"But who will travel with you? Who will accompany you on the rabab? Who will be your scribe and note down your songs?"

"Yes, that is pretty serious, Mardana. Let us pray that something happens between now and the butcher's blade. God's treasuries are never empty. He keeps on giving for generations and generations. He gives so much that receivers get tired of receiving. So, goats, let us pray."

"What about them?" they asked, pointing at Razaa and the other women. "They won't let us stop and pray."

"We can pray as we walk."

"No, no, I would rather stop and pray," Mardana stalled.

"Let me ask them," said Baba.

"Don't!" Mardana whispered. "They will turn you into a goat, too. Then you will be sacrificed, and who will tell our families that the outcome of all our wanderings and journeys was to be slaughtered and eaten?"

Baba chuckled to himself and then said, "If that is how God wants us to end up, that's how it will be. It's all written, Mardana. It is written on your horns! See? 'To be sacrificed to the goddess Maya.'"

"Please free us!" the goats bleated pitifully.

"Let's see what can be done," Baba said. "I do want my rababi back. I can't tell you how much I have missed you, Mardana!"

Mardana's heart leaped so high with joy he felt it would kill him. Just to hear Baba say that was enough. It was more than enough. His life had been wildly successful. He was happy—no, ecstatic—to die.

"Listen," Baba said to the women who were leading the goats. They stopped, turned around, and looked at Baba with amazement. Their first exclamations were, "Another sacrifice for the goddess! How pleased she will be if we bring an extra goat!"

"Sisters, I have come to seek the release of my rababi," Baba said.

"What about us, what about us?" the others bleated. "Seek our release, too."

"Release!" the women cried, smiling the smiles that had made Mardana and his fellow goats lose their heads in the first place. Their red lips, moistened with the juice of the *kusumb*[1] flower, were parted most seductively as their *kajaled*[2] eyes, liquid with passion and the deep promise of unbound pleasure, looked into Baba's. They stood with their slender hands on their well-shaped hips in poses that accentuated their full, firm, youthful breasts, bare ankles, shapely feet, and exposed midriffs in *cholis* and *ghagras*.

Baba stood firmly and continued to look at them with eyes that pierced through their appearances to their souls. They looked at Baba, at his dark, thick beard with a few streaks of gray; the glow on his handsome face; his eyes at once gentle, astute, and discerning; and they felt a resistance that only made them double their efforts to gain this prize.

But Baba remained unmoved. The women huddled amongst themselves in bewilderment. Could this be the man their mistress, Nur Shah, would succumb to, they wondered, both fearing and hoping for such an eventuality. They feared that life as they knew it, the familiar purpose of keeping themselves forever young, would crumble and collapse; yet they also hoped for a new life filled with love, something they had never experienced. No, they concluded; this was too remote a possibility. Such a man did not exist. Hundreds of thousands had come, and all of them had succumbed to temptation.

"Take me to your mistress, maidens," Baba said.

"Don't, Baba," Mardana whispered. "Not her. I have heard such stories about her. We are both doomed if we go to her. Work one of your miracles."

"He is right," Taakat concurred. "No one can resist her."

Mardana shuddered in fear. Baba Nanak put his hand on Mardana's neck and patted him with an affectionate and reassuring caress, and they started their climb up the spiraling hill to Nur Shah's fortress and temple.

---

[1] Safflower, whose color is impermanent. Used as a symbol of the fleeting and illusory phenomenon of life. Invariably contrasted with madder, whose color is permanent.

[2] Heavily lined with black.

"Baba," said Mardana, straining and bucking on his tether as they climbed up the craggy, rocky path. "Don't underestimate her power. There is danger here. No one has ever escaped her. Just make a miracle; turn us into men with an incantation, and we will kill these witches."

"I know there is danger here," Baba replied. "Maya and her charms are irresistible to all, including me. Even the best succumb and fall, but I know no miracles, Mardana. We shall have to leave it all to the Immaculate One. Let us pray in our hearts that we overcome her seductions and that we do not get ourselves enmeshed and strangled in her colorful, magical web."

"I can tell you that all your prayers are useless when it comes to Nur Shah's power," Taakat said. "All you have to do is look at her, and you are doomed. Should you survive—and that is very unlikely—you will end up touching the witch, which will seal your fate."

CHAPTER 15
The Fortress

Standing on the battlement of her fortress, Nur Shah saw the bound goats climbing the hill, but her temper flared when she saw the man walking with them. What was a human doing in her kingdom? Of course, it meant another goat for the sacrifice, but why had they not turned him into a goat already? Why were they bringing him to her residence, instead of to the temple? Nur Shah didn't want to be bothered by the menial task of turning men into goats. This was a bad sign. Were their powers failing them? Was it the beginning of the end?

Nur Shah's stone heart was gripped with fear as she remembered the prophecy: when the one who can't be transformed into a goat arrives, you will die and crumble into dust unless you surrender to him. This Nur Shah would never do, for it would mean the end of her power, and yet, the deep, dark recesses of her heart longed for such a man. How many lifetimes had she waited for the one she could surrender to entirely? The one to whom she would give everything she had—all her possessions, wealth, beauty, power—and become his slave? Could he be the one?

For a brief moment, the dry tinder of Nur Shah's heart caught a spark, but it died almost instantly. *Centuries have gone by. It cannot be. I am doomed to live alone forever, locked away in this tower of stone.*

Hope turned to ash. This man would be like all the other men—lustful and oh so seducible. No, the man who could resist her existed only in her dreams.

That dream vision had recurred often since her adolescence: a path in a dark and frightening forest teeming with wild animals, ominous birds overhead. Then the sudden appearance of a being, his form and eyes casting circles of light that dispelled the pitch black of night. In the dream she would always think, *It is the prince come to rescue me! He will carry me away on his white horse!* But he always vanished, leaving her bereft, the pain in her heart so intense it would awaken her. After every such dream she would vow never to love any man, those abominably weak creatures. She would only love a man who did not succumb to her beauty, and such a man did not exist.

Ashes, ashes, Nur Shah thought, turning away and entering the luxurious bedroom of her stronghold. She lay listlessly on her bed, weary, the ice in her heart hardening. She derived no pleasure or comfort from any of the things that she had been so passionate about earlier: her lovely body preserved with magical herbs and the blood and brains of goat men, the beneficence of Goddess Maya's joy at the continual sacrifices, her domain that extended as far as the eye could see, and her castles, palaces, jewelry, wealth, and slaves.

Nur Shah felt her skin tightening like a shroud, squeezing out her breath, as if the walls of her fortress were collapsing upon her, and all its doors were tightly locked with not a chink or pore remaining for escape. She was trapped within herself, and her life had become a curse. The thought of a man superior to her only produced fear and loathing in her heart.

She got up again and looked at her reflections in the many mirrors of her room, mirrors that had previously delighted her and before which she had spent many a pleasant hour. She looked at her legendary youthful features, vibrant, flowing hair, sensuous, blood-red lips, and kohl-rimmed eyes, drawing all hungry men in. Yes, she was exquisite—except for a brilliant hardness the mirror reflected. Though her face was unnaturally youthful, her heart was like a fruit that has decayed from within while still holding on to the hope of being consumed. As she looked at herself, Nur Shah's confidence in her own power returned and held her fear in check.

She went back to the parapet to watch the human accompanying the goats. She watched his strong, lithe body beneath a flowing *chola*;[1] his dark, bushy beard on an intent face; his gait at once carefree and strong; his long arms swaying as he walked with what looked like a musical instrument strung on his shoulder, and her heart flared with desire and fear.

---

[1] A long robe worn by men that falls below the knees.

By then Baba Nanak, accompanied by the goats, had reached the massive obsidian gates of Nur Shah's marble fortress. He rang all the large bronze bells that hung upon them, announcing his arrival. The gates flung open, and Baba stepped in. When the goats tried to follow Baba into the castle, the women said, "No goats inside!"

The goats bleated loudly, some standing on their hind legs, kicking in protest, knowing that once Baba entered the gates they would be taken to the temple and slaughtered before Baba could save them. Though they didn't think it probable, they still hoped that Baba would perform a miracle to rescue them.

"I will not go in without them," Baba said.

The girls laughed cruelly. "These smelly, filthy things—inside?"

It took only one glance from Baba for the girls to begin relaying the message to Nur Shah.

"Goats," Baba said, holding up his rabab as if it were a weapon, "Prepare for battle."

"What—without weapons or hands, with only our butting heads and horns?"

"You have the greatest weapon of all—consciousness. It was given to you at the time of your embodiment into flesh. The enemy is . . . "

"We all know who the enemy is," Taakat said tersely.

"It is not Nur Shah," Baba said.

"Maya, then, whose priestess she is?"

"The enemy is your mind, which allows itself to get caught in the illusions of Nur Shah and Maya and turns you into goats. The uncontrolled mind is a mad animal running wildly in your home. Unless it is trained to submit its small understanding to consciousness, it destroys both the house and the person within it."

"How can we learn to do this, Baba?" Mannay asked.

"By asking for help from the only agency that can help; by carrying the lamp of remembrance in our hearts."

Baba's words and voice created a deep calm in the goats.

The girls were back and they shouted, "The goats must stay outside!"

"Then I will stay outside too," Baba said. The girls ran to relay the message to their mistress.

Baba sat on the ground, and the goats gathered around him in a circle. "Let us pray that our minds stay still in the midst of the storm that awaits us."

"Baba, even *you* feel desire? Even *you* can be tempted by Nur Shah's wiles?" Mannay asked.

"I am also an animal and experience all the appetites. Come, join me as I sing."

"But will God understand the singing of goats?"

"God understands all sorts of singing." Baba smiled.

As the rabab sprang alive in his hands, a deep chord of soulful, harmonic overtones spread in concentric circles. It seemed to the goats that even the stone walls of the fortress were humming along with their own vibrating cells as Baba sang:

> Man ray thir rahu mat kat jaahee jee-o;
> baahar dhoodhat bahut dukh paavahi,
> ghar amrit ghat maahee jee-o.
> (O my mind, be still;
> wandering here and there you suffer great pain,
> sweet nectar is found in your own home.)

Baba's lingering, lyrical notes, at once free and restrained, reverberated in their hearts. Even the girls stopped their relay race to Nur Shah and stood transfixed by a new feeling—a stillness and a movement within it like the silent unfolding of a swan's wings. Everything else ceased, and only the sensation of the rippling sounds remained, like a whisper of blissful eternity. The goats had never heard anything like this in Mardana's singing. Even gruff, tough Taakat came under the spell of Baba's voice; his ever-active brain quieted down as he experienced existence in a new way. The self-righteous, constricted Sidda felt the encrustations in his soul loosening and crumbling. Mannay was in ecstasy. Even Nur Shah in her chamber heard the echoing words and for the briefest of moments forgot her battle mode, her armor falling away as she panicked. *It is him!* This thought frightened her terribly, for love, which demands the annihilation of the self, an expansion of boundaries to include others, and a surrender of strength, is the most frightening of emotions. Fearing that surrendering to this man, who had such passion and compassion in his voice, would turn her into a docile, will-less sheep, she exerted her prodigious willpower, shut her ears to the sound, and prepared for battle. She would show him. Her ringing command echoed through the marble palace walls as the message went out: "Let them all come in."

CHAPTER 16
Grinding Wheels

With the still-humming rabab slung on his shoulder, Baba entered the wide portal and stepped on a floor inlaid with intricate patterns of gold and precious stones. With the pitter-patter of hooves behind him, and the goats' constant commentary of "Look, look!" "Isn't that luscious?" "This is amazing!" and "I want that!" Baba walked unimpressed through corridors and rooms made of gold brick walls and columns of exquisitely carved ivory.

They stepped into a large hall, its circular walls so transparent that they could see beyond them into vistas of palaces, castles, and fortresses, each with wide courtyards containing armies of soldiers, horses, elephants, and chariots—all the paraphernalia of extreme power and wealth. The goats gaped, amazed at how huge Nur Shah's kingdom truly was.

Baba stood at the very center of the round hall, while the goats surrounded him in a circle.

"What's happening?" Mardana said, losing his balance. "The whole floor is moving like a spinning wheel! And look there, another wheel next to this one! It's whirling, too!"

"There are three!" cried Sidda.

"Four, five, six, ten!" said Taakat.

"There's only one, but it appears as many," Baba said.

"Look! Look! No, don't look, don't look! There are deep pits with meat grinders that separate the wheels. I'm falling, Baba; I am slipping and sliding into it! I'm falling, help me!"

"Mardana, breathe deeply and remember the name with each breath. It will help you stay still in the midst of this whirling. The wheels are an illusion, but they can kill you. No matter what happens, *do not move*."

Baba had barely finished speaking when the wheels began to grind fast and furiously to a terrible cacophony, grating and gyrating beneath them. On each of the wheels Baba and the goats saw visions of themselves in terrifying and pleasant scenarios. Mardana saw a vision of his house, with Fatima sitting by the fire cooking a feast for him, while his children and grandchildren sat and played in the courtyard, and his dog, Moti, barked and came toward him, wagging his tail fiercely. Mardana was sorely tempted to enter the scene.

"These scenes are mirrors of your mind, traps to catch and bind your souls. They will arouse desires and fears, but do not prefer one over the other, nor judge between pleasure and pain, good and evil. Stay detached from both, or you will perish." Though Baba did not shout these words above the deafening dissonance, each goat heard them clearly, as if from within his own heart.

"They are phantoms of your brain, thought forms that collude with desire to create illusions," Baba continued. "It is a drama staged in a dream."

"But they seem so real!" the goats cried.

"Everything you see is a creation of the great architect of the world, Maya. Do not take it for real; do not identify with any part of it."

Soon, other images assaulted the goats, fearful images that they instinctively wanted to flee.

"But I have a choice, don't I, of going there instead of here?" Mardana asked, trying desperately to steady himself.

"You are deluded into thinking you have a choice. Give the choice to the All Knowing, All Seeing. Be patient and content while He shows you the way. Wait trustingly."

Fortunately, Mardana recalled all the crises he had ended up in every time he turned a deaf ear to Baba's words and resolved to obey. Though his desire compelled him to move toward scenes in which he was rich, famous, and powerful and away from terrifying and loathsome scenes in which he saw himself dismembered, dead, or dying, he remained still. The goats who did not heed

Baba's words and moved either toward or away from an image were crushed by the wheels; others were caught between opposing forces so intense that they were torn in two but still lived; some jumped to safety from perceived dangers and perished.

Mardana saw a pool with water hot as fire, flames and steam rising from it. He saw Fatima and his children, sinking and calling out to him for help in heartrending cries, like those of animals in pain.

"I can't bear it! I want to be with them! I'm going to help them!"

"Maya is appealing to your good nature, but it is a trick and a temptation, Mardana. Those are the scalding waters of emotional attachment, in which many build their homes and drown."

"But there is so much tension, so much suffering!" Mardana wept.

"Bear it consciously."

"But . . . " Mardana's words frayed as he found himself spinning around furiously. Baba caught him by his tail, pulled it hard, and said, "Stay still! Remember Allah, you fool!"

Baba's tone was so harsh and urgent that Mardana knew this was no time to doubt. Everything depended upon it. He prayed earnestly, "I am a weak fool and cannot stay still. Help me and let me surrender to your will, Allah!"

Almost immediately, Mardana felt calm and found the strength to be still and centered. He tore his eyes away from the scene and kept them firmly fixed on Baba's feet. Mannay, too, kept the flame of God's name enshrined in his heart as a talisman against dangers; Taakat, impressed by Baba's calm and peaceful face, knew in his heart that Baba's method was sound and followed his advice. Sidda, however, saw himself as the high priest of a large and imposing temple with people genuflecting to him, an image of power that was so dear to his heart that he moved toward it and was ground into meat between the wheels.

Throughout all of this Baba stood still, eyes closed, his fingers strumming the *sa-pa* chord on the rabab, absorbed in that one sound that anchored him to God and reminded him to stay above the horrible and the pleasurable, the fear of death and the desire for life. The vibrations shielded the goats that took shelter in the sound. After what seemed like an eternity, the wheels appeared to stop and all was calm and silent.

"It's over! It's over, Baba, you won!" Mardana said.

"There's no winning or losing, only being awake and vigilant," Baba said. Before he had finished uttering these words, the scene changed entirely. The air around them became soft and fragrant with incense, illumined with candlelight and filled with sensuous and lovely music. The goats, exhausted from their ordeal, sighed in relief and were ready to sink into the soft comfort of pleasure, when Nur Shah herself appeared, accompanied by the heady fragrance of musk, indescribable in her beauty and allure beneath a diaphanous veil that revealed as much as it concealed. The goats could see tantalizing glimpses of her luscious curves in the fullness of womanhood, her lips provocative with the juice of the *kusumb* flower, her large eyes, outlined with kohl, sloshing over with the pent-up desire of a lifetime. She walked toward them with a beguiling smile on her face, the sound of her ankle bells so seductive that all present were inclined to surrender themselves to her, body, mind, and soul. She reclined on a soft, silken couch and opened her arms wide. It seemed to each goat that all the other goats vanished, and she spoke and beckoned to him alone.

"Isn't she irresistible?" Mardana whispered to Baba.

"Yes, oh yes," Baba said. "I don't blame you for what you did, Mardana, for even I can barely resist the attraction of her magic."

"I could become a double goat for that," Mardana said. "How can you refuse, Baba?"

"Because I don't want to end up as you did. Desire has consequences."

"You, you are the winner," Nur Shah said in gentle, musical speech, and to each she proffered a golden chalice of wine. "You are my hero. You are the one! I have waited for you for so long. Come to me, and I will give you eternal life!"

Each present felt extreme thirst at the sight of the chalice. Each goat extended an arm—an illusory human arm—to reach for it.

"It is the wine of Maya, fleeting in its effect. Don't abandon the ambrosia of the Friend's name for it!" Baba warned.

To those goats who had learned nothing from their previous ordeals, Baba's words, almost like an inaudible whisper, seemed insipid and pale compared to the scene before them. They were proud of themselves for withstanding the grinding wheels, for becoming (they thought) men again. Convinced that they fully deserved the prize Nur Shah offered them, they grasped the golden chalice, ready to quaff its contents to quench their extreme thirst. The chalices crumbled in their hands, and they collapsed into heaps of dust and ashes that were whisked away by the wind.

For those who listened to Baba's words and refused the chalice, Nur Shah changed her tactics. In a cloudburst of thunder and lightning she morphed into the dreaded Kali with a garland of human skulls around her neck, a bloody sword in hand, her bloody tongue thrust out of her charred and black-ened face, and eyes that struck such terror into the goats' hearts that they were ready to flee.

"Don't run away from her," Baba warned. The goats saw a chasm behind them and were glad they had heeded Baba's warning.

When Nur Shah's tactics failed to move Baba and those who took shelter in his words, everything became calm and still. A sob was heard in the silence, and Nur Shah cried with genuine feeling.

"I feel again. After centuries, I *feel* again. You, *you* are the One for whom I have waited for centuries. You are finally here! I admit defeat. Take all of me!" Nur Shah said to Baba.

"It's another of her tricks," Taakat whispered to Baba. "Don't listen to her. Now is the time to attack and kill her. She is close enough."

"She's just trying to get you to touch her!" Mardana said.

But Baba's eyes were locked into hers, and he didn't listen to them.

"Be mine. Take me; take everything I have, only be mine. Never leave me! We can have love beyond the experience of mortals, an ever-passionate and undying love."

It seemed to the goats that Baba was going through a tremendous inner struggle. Leaving his rabab on the floor, he took one step toward Nur Shah.

"Take all this," Nur Shah continued, sweeping her hands at the slave girls, the palace, the vast vistas of her kingdom, "and love me in return!"

Baba took another step. All was lost now, and the goats dropped pellets in fear. Baba struggled to keep from moving, yet his body moved with a will of its own, as if propelled by some magic power. He took another step. There was tremendous tension in his muscles, as if they were kept in check by a supreme effort of will. Then suddenly he relaxed, as though he had surren-dered himself entirely to the will of a power that kept him still and rooted to his center. He was relaxed the way a tuned string is at once relaxed and taut enough to play the note at its perfect pitch. He retraced his steps, picked up the rabab, cradled it to his chest, and sat down on the floor. The goats, tired from their experiences, collapsed near him. Baba ran his fingers tenderly, lovingly over the body of the rabab and began to hum the first notes of an alaap so soulful, so sweet, and with such compelling feeling that it flowed out like a river of cool water over hot, dry sands. He shut his eyes, turned in to himself, and returning to the inner castle where he communed with his Beloved, strummed the rabab. So wonderful was the sound after such turbulence in the soul that a deep calm descended on all. Mardana knew that bani had come to Baba, that his chaos had turned to consonance. The first notes of Baba's alaap, and the first few lines, flowing out of him with such heartfelt longing, reassured Mardana that all was well.

Mottee tan mandar ossarai,
ratnee tan hohi jaraoo.

"If I had a palace," Baba sang, elaborating on the images in the refrain, "inlaid with jewels, scented with musk, saffron, and sandalwood, a sheer delight to behold; if the floor of the palace was a mosaic of diamonds and rubies and my bed encased with jewels; if heavenly beauties adorned with emeralds enticed me with sensual pleasures, your Name wouldn't enter my mind, and I would forget You, my Beloved, and my soul would be scorched to ash."

Agonized, Nur Shah cried, "I have found you and lost you to God!"

Baba stood up and moved toward her. He reached out an arm to Nur Shah, and the goats trembled and panicked again—but they need not have feared. Baba reached for Nur Shah's veil and with one movement of his hand stripped it clean away. With one piercing glance, he saw through the alluring illusion of Nur Shah's beauty and youth and into her true nature. A collective scream from the other enchantresses pierced the air as all gasped at what they saw.

A doddering old woman—her face like pale, flaking parchment; eyes sunken into cavernous, bony sockets; her scalp bald with a few stray gray hairs; and her corpselike body the color of ash—stood before them. A similar transformation took place in all the other girls: their rich clothes turned to rags, and their youthful faces turned into the visages of hags, on which their makeup stood like hideous masks. The eyes of these crumbling women on the verge of disintegration were still bright with burning desire.

"What's happening? Where are my herbs? Where is my makeup? Where is my kohl? Where are my colors?" Nur Shah screamed in a high-pitched, shaky voice. "And where is my fortress? What's happened to my gardens, my land?"

Together with Nur Shah's transformation, everything—the castle and its opulent riches, the courtyard, the fortress, the armies, and the chariots—vanished like a phantasmagoric dream, as if Baba, with that one movement, had torn through the entire illusion of Maya's magic. The trees turned to desolate skeletons, and all that remained in the distance were the pens where all the men whom Nur Shah had changed into goats were bleating mournfully, tethered to their stakes.

"What's happening? What have you done to me?" Nur Shah sobbed in anguish.

"I have only shown you the condition of your heart. For as our hearts are, so we become. Your colors were the color of the *kusumb* flower, whose redness is like a fading dream in the night. Go, put your heart where, unbeknownst to you, it longs to be, and He will dye you in the unfading madder[1] of His love."

"I don't want some abstract thing to love, I want you! *You* are the One," Nur Shah cried, her eyes burning with disappointment. "I want you in my life, in my heart, in my bed, and in my kingdom. Stay and bring my heart back to life!" Nur Shah, a vulnerable and weak creature without her armor of wealth, beauty, youth, and power, fell at Baba's feet. To all present, her youthful passion seemed incongruous with her disintegrating body, fallen into a heap of brittle bones and crumbling flesh.

"Child," he said, in gentle words full of love, "do not fall in love with one who is destined to leave; my body is dust; the wind speaks through it. You think your search has been for me, but I am just an instrument of your search for the True One. We are always looking for the Beloved, even through all of our small, insignificant searches. Only the One can absorb the vastness of our desires in an insatiable and ever-intensifying passion. His love is constant, deathless, not subject to the vagaries and confusions of human love. He is the eternal Groom and we the eternal brides. That supreme Love alone is worthy of all our love, child."

---

[1] A permanent red dye, used as a symbol of truth.

"But I do not want to die without having known human love! Each bird and beast, insect and fly has its mate, but not me! You have made me mortal—now fulfill my human needs to have someone to whom I am dear, someone to hold, and talk to, so I may speak my heart!"

The girls were weeping copiously as Nur Shah's words echoed in the cold, empty caverns of their own hearts.

"I am powerless to change your fate. Pray to Him who can do it in his mercy."

"I don't know anything about prayers!"

"Prayers are nothing but love, child. If you want love, then learn to love."

Baba shut his eyes, and his face softened in such an intense way that Mardana knew bani was coming again. Baba reached for his rabab and began.

> Man ray, kyon chootai bin pyaar?
> (O my mind, how will you be saved without Love?
> He abides within His lover and gives him the world.)

As Baba instructed them through his song how to love, the bare rods of the trees began to bud. Tiny green shoots began to unfurl into the blue air. Nur Shah and the girls were weeping in torrents, and their weeping was like rain in deserts that had been dry for millennia. A dark, live sorrow, a sense of regret, shame, and guilt at their cold, wasted, and soiled lives stirred in the ashes of their hearts. Death, which they had kept at bay with their magic, entered their consciousness, and in its wake hope returned, for death alone bestows life and feeling, beauty and love.

"But will He love this . . . this unclean thing?" Nur Shah asked.

"The body is cleansed with soap and water; the soul is cleansed with the Pure One's name. If He so wills, He can dissolve millions upon millions of sins in an instant."

"I don't even know where to begin!"

"A large pile of firewood burns with a small spark."

"But I am so old and ugly! Look how my kohl has smeared around my eyes and run down my face!"

Baba wiped her face with his hand and said, "*Gyaan anjan*, the kohl of knowledge and wisdom will make you beautiful again, and it will not be a beauty that fades."

Baba turned around and began to walk down the hill. Stripped of its fantastical elements it was just a simple, lovely hill with greening shrubs and large boulders. The goats were amazed at the drama that had unfolded before their eyes. Baba went to the pens, which were loud with lamentations, and opened the doors wide. Sunlight flooded the darkness in which the goats lay and stood, covered in their own filth. He untied each of them and released the nooses around their necks. The rumor that Baba had changed their captors into helpless old women soon spread amongst them, and a collective bleat went up in jubilation. The goats jostled to get into the sunshine, then blinked in confusion. Where was the scene that had so captivated them? Where were the huts and the fortresses, the feasting and merriment of beautiful women? Was it all magic, a construct of their brains? The only reminders of it were their furry legs and the hooves on which they followed Nanak as he strode ahead of them, his steps strong and certain, the rabab strung on his shoulder.

CHAPTER 17
Lord of Desire

L eaping, kicking, and rejoicing, the goats followed Baba Nanak, hoping
that soon the magic would wear off and they would all revert to being
men again. But no such thing happened.

They proceeded farther on their journey into a dark forest. Hungry lions
roared and growled in the distance, and the goats became aware of their vul-
nerability. They had been rescued from Nur Shah only to fall into the mouths
of other predators.

"Baba!" cried the goats. "We are all still goats! We still have horns and
hooves."

"You'll have to learn to become men again then, won't you?" Baba replied.

"But how do we begin? We've had no control over what has happened to
us since we strayed into Nur Shah's clutches. There was nothing we could
do against such bewitchment. You yourself experienced her power and know
what we mean. We don't have your supernatural powers. We are not to blame!"

"As long as you keep thinking this way, you will continue to be goats,"
Baba said in his soft but firm voice. "The first step to becoming human
is realizing your own responsibility in what happens to you. Your lust
created this experience. You eat what you sow. You pray for fulfillment
of your desires, your wishes come true, and they are only what you have
feared all along."

"If God wanted us to be celibate, he would have made us so, then we would have been content. He gives us sexuality and tells us not to be sexual!" a goat grumbled.

"To be with one woman is celibacy," Baba said.

"You said he was a powerful sage," another goat said to Mardana. "You said he could make humans into angels, but he can't even make animals into humans. What good is he?"

"You ungrateful wretch!" Mardana, spurred to Baba's defense, screamed as he locked horns with the goat. "He has just released you from death!"

"But what good is it? We are easy game for these roaring lions that will hunt, slaughter, and eat us!"

Mannay shouted above the din of the arguments. "Help us, Baba! We are blind. Be our eyes, show us the way, and teach us how to be men. Please!"

The goats surrounded Baba Nanak in a circle, pleading and bleating. Baba sat cross-legged on the grass while the goats congregated around him in a circle. A sweet, gentle, and cleansing rain began to fall. Mardana trotted over to Baba Nanak and sat down beside him in the place he usually took when accompanying him on the rabab.

"I don't understand, Baba," Mardana said, humbly. "You always say God is the Doer—only what He wills, happens. So how can we be responsible for what happens to us?"

"You're letting your mind get in the way of your understanding, Mardana. Think with your heart, and you'll understand how we can be responsible *and* submissive. Admit that you were inattentive to what was happening in your mind before Nur Shah's girls captured you. Thoughts are real, and they make you what you are."

"What shall we do? How shall we think? How can we keep our minds from getting in the way of our understanding?" Mannay asked.

"The manmukh mind, the mind that faces the ego, is the mind that gets in the way of our understanding and leads us astray. Unless the manmukh mind is controlled, Maya will delude us into pursuing what is unreal and what can only cause suffering. It is this self-willed, fickle, ever-changing mind, continuously running after fleeting things, that leads us astray on the path of life, imprisons us in the pen of the sorceress, Maya, and destroys us. But if we tame the mind, we conquer and inherit the world."

"We have to rein, harness, and ride the manmukh mind," Mardana said, a glimmer of understanding sparking his brain.

"What shall I do with my mind after I harness it?" a goat asked, as if doing this was an easy task.

Baba smiled and said, "Give it away."

"To whom?" Mardana asked.

"To its Owner, Mardana. Surrender the horse of your mind to its Creator who knows best, and who will guide it in the right direction."

"I don't understand. How shall I live without my mind?" a confused goat asked.

"Oh, it will return to you, undoubtedly. It will return as the gurmukh mind, the mind that is turned inward, toward God. It will return knowing more than it knows now, knowing you must give all your desires to God to fulfill or to squash. When you learn to sit still in the center of your swirling desires, it will return as the mind of a true Sikh."[1]

"Baba, what or who is a Sikh?"

"A Sikh is a devotee and disciple of God, a student who is always eager and passionate to learn how to grow into his full potential as a true and conscious human being."

"And how can I become a Sikh?"

"By keeping your vessel upright," Baba said, taking his *lota* from his bag, clearing the space before him, and standing the *lota* upside down upon the ground. "Nothing can be contained in a vessel turned upside down. But if you straighten it," he said, doing so, "ambrosia will fall into it."

"How does one keep one's vessel upright?"

"With humility. When we are humble, when we give all our possessions and ourselves to our Maker, knowing that all is His anyway, then He himself keeps our vessel upright."

"How do we even know there is a God?" a skeptical goat asked.

"Formless water is confined within the pitcher, but without water, the pitcher could not have been formed," Baba said, enigmatically.

Some goats looked perplexed by Baba's answer. To them, he explained, "Doubt, duality, and separation are Maya's greatest illusions. They arise in the mind separated from the Source."

---

[1] The word *sikh* goes back to the Sanskrit *sisya*, meaning a learner or disciple. The Punjabi form of the word is *sikh*, a pupil.

"I'm afraid if I give everything to God, he will quash all my desires and give me a crust of bread," a goat said.

"If you give your life to God, God gives you the world," Baba said. "God is the Lord of Desire. Beg from the One Lord, the Great Giver, and you shall obtain your heart's desires."

"Will God fulfill our desires even for things like wealth, property, fame, fortune, homes, wives, and children? These things are very important to me," an honest goat admitted.

"One who loves the Lord obtains the fruit of that love; all his hunger is satisfied. To the gurmukh, everything is sacred and pure—food, drink, wealth, property, and money. He is a happy man, fully at home with all aspects of life, tasting all the pleasures, knowing that God Himself is the giver of them, that God enjoys Himself through the gurmukh's joy in life. God is a yogi, an ascetic, and a *bhogi*, an enjoyer. Among pleasure seekers, he is a pleasure seeker; among the ascetics, he is an ascetic. The gurmukh enjoys it all, but is not attached to any of it. He doesn't eat the fly together with the sweets."

Baba reached for his rabab, and everyone fell silent. The strings pulsated with vibrations and waves that encompassed everything—the goats, trees, grass, sky, setting sun, and dirt. Baba began his alaap and sang in a dulcet voice filled with holy passion.

Aapay rasee-aa aap ras aapay ravanhaar.
Aapay hovai cholrhaa aapay sayj bhataar.

"He himself is the bride in her dress," Baba sang. "He himself is the bridegroom on the bed; he himself is the enjoyer, the enjoyment, and the joy."

Baba's voice was steeped in divine ecstasy, and he sang as if in a trance till the last note merged into silence. The goats were swept up in an oceanic, cosmic feeling that healed their wounded hearts and their torn minds, which were so accustomed to thinking in a choppy, fragmented, divisive, and dualistic way.

A sudden movement interrupted the quiet that followed Baba's singing, and everyone sat amazed at the sight before them. Mannay the goat stood unsteadily on two legs. His fur fell off his body like a coat, his cloven hooves morphed into hands and legs, his muzzle and mouth shortened into a human face, and his horns and tail disappeared. He soon stood before them as an upright man in all his glory.

As the goats cried in amazement, Mannay himself was calm, though very moved. He fell at Baba's feet, and Baba put his hand on his head.

"How did you do it? What did you do? How did this happen?" The goats crowded around him.

"I listened; I obeyed," Mannay replied.

"Not fair," one of the goats grumbled, turning to Baba. "Make us men, too!"

Mardana found an old jealousy stirring in him, but on its heels came a vision so encompassing that it nipped that feeling in the bud. All the things Baba had said to him hitherto that he had imbibed subconsciously suddenly bloomed in his consciousness with crystal clarity. He knew and felt that everything Baba said was true and right and good and beautiful and utterly practical; Baba was the guru he trusted without reservations and conditions. Henceforth, Baba would be Mardana's eyes, his support, and the voice in his conscience that would guide him for whatever remained of his life. It was Baba's magic he wanted now, not Maya's. He felt awakened from a long sleep. A door opened, and Mardana leapt into the Beloved's welcoming heart with arms wide open. He knew, even as he experienced the most intense feeling of his life, that though he would fall from this place again and again, this would be the post and the stake to which he would return over and over as he moved through his days. This would be the center, the very core of his being. He also knew that he didn't create this expansive feeling; that it was grace, like rain in his soul.

"Mardanaia, rabab chhaid, Bhai."

Mardana extended his arm and received the rabab. *What a miracle to have hands*, Mardana thought. *What a miracle to be a man! What an opportunity that I had almost lost!*

His fingers touched the rabab as if it were a beloved after an insufferably long separation: gently, with love, with gratitude, and with tears. All Mardana's senses concentrated into that one vibrating sound that always had the power to align his body, mind, and soul into a synergy, transporting him to the one place where all his senses were at once active and at rest. The world became vibrant, pulsating with energy. He and the sound became one, his whole awareness concentrated in the singing and vibrating string.

Too aap bhulaaveh naam visaar.
Too aapay raakhahi kirpaa Dhaar.

"You yourself cause us to stray from the path and forget naam," Mardana sang along with Baba in a voice reborn after a long silence. "Showering your mercy, you yourself save us."

CHAPTER 18
City of God

S o Baba set out with the goats-turned-men and the goats that hoped to become men in tow. They eventually arrived at a vast expanse of land by the wide Ravi River.

Mardana said, looking all around him, "If I had money, Baba, I would buy this tract of land for us. My desire for a nice home with a little bit of land to cultivate is raging."

"Maybe, Mardana, the Bestower will fulfill your desire."

They set up camp by a ramshackle, abandoned hut with a partial roof. Baba's followers put a thatch on it, and a few others cleared a spot by the roots of the large, spreading banyan tree beneath which Baba often sat, singing and discoursing. Baba's erstwhile goat followers, who had gone to visit their families, returned with wives and children, mothers and fathers, cattle, bulls, buffalo, and dogs, and before they knew it, a little hutment had sprung up around Baba and Mardana.

Meanwhile the wealthy person—so wealthy that he called himself *Karoria*, meaning the billionaire—to whom the land belonged began to hear news of a famous fakir who had been camping on his land. Many of his subjects left his township to serve the fakir, and stories spread of healings and transformations.

Though he owned so much land that the small portion Baba Nanak and his disciples occupied was but a drop in the ocean of his possessions, Karoria grew enraged at him. How dare he take any portion of his land! How dare this sham god-man lure his subjects away from him with pretense and quackery?

Karoria called his trusted advisor, Amir Shah, and ordered him to go to the encampment with his army and evict the imposter who had stolen his land and his popularity.

Amir Shah bowed and set out to do his bidding. Karoria waited for the happy news with impatience, but when Amir Shah did not return for several days, he grew angry again. When Amir Shah returned with only a few members of the army to report that the rest of the men had stayed back and worshipped Baba instead of evicting him, Karoria was beside himself with fury.

Determined to put an end to the occupation, Karoria asked Amir to get his favorite Arabian horse, Sohji, from the stables. She was his favorite because whenever Karoria was lost in the uncharted jungles where he often went hunting, he would slacken her reins, and she would unerringly take him in the right direction, guiding him when he came to a crossroads and bringing him home safely.

Karoria patted the well-caparisoned horse lovingly on the rump, leaped upon her with power and strength, and spurred her gently. Sohji did not budge. He spurred her harder, to no avail.

"What's the matter with you? You have never done this before. Are you sick?" The veterinarian was called, and after checking her out thoroughly, he pronounced Sohji in excellent health.

Karoria mounted her once more and spurred her hard. Sohji neighed, shied, and bucked so violently that Karoria fell off and was trampled under one of her hooves. He was carried groaning and moaning to his bed, where he was laid up for several days.

Rumors flew that Karoria's horse was an enlightened being and people began to worship her, bringing her carrots, sugar, rice cakes, and the choicest of hays, and putting garlands of marigolds and jasmine around her neck and ears.

Feeling a bit better, Karoria resolved to do battle again. Sohji was readied, and he mounted her again. Just when he had settled into the saddle, Karoria began to rub his eyes and shout, "I can't see; my eyes, my eyes, I'm going blind!"

He was carried into his house once more. The best doctors were called, and all of them were baffled by Karoria's sudden affliction. None of them could cure him. Karoria, laid up in bed again, became more and more jealous of Baba's popularity. His jealousy grew to such a pitch that he began to dream deliriously. In a lucid moment he sent for Amir and cried, "Amir! Something dreadful has happened in a corner of my land! I want to destroy it before it destroys me!"

Then Karoria proceeded to tell Amir his dreams, one fragment at a time, and asked him for his interpretations.

"The fakir wrestled with me all night, and when I plunged my sword into him, it was I, Karoria, who was wounded and lay dying on the battlefield."

Amir cleared his throat and said, "*Hazoor,*[1] you were not wrestling with Baba Nanak, but with yourself. Your ego self is fighting with your higher self, and the former is being defeated."

"But he killed me, and I died in my dream! As I lay under my shroud, people came crowding into my house and took everything away from me! A man even pulled my ring, this ring, from my finger—and took my finger along with it! Then demons and goblins bound, gagged, and dragged me away and put me on a pyre!"

Amir resolved, after all these years, to speak his mind. He saw that unless he did so, there was no chance of his master's recovery.

"To dream of death means some part of our old self, our ego, needs to die. Sometimes we have to die to be reborn, hazoor. Baba Nanak says the world is a bubble made of a drop of rain; everything that is seen shall pass away. Everything in it belongs to the Creator. Nothing—not our wealth, or even our minds and our bodies—is ours. You have forgotten your death, hazoor."

Karoria was shocked at Amir's manner of speaking. He was about to scold him, when he remembered another fragment of his dream.

"When I looked up from the pyre, the flames engulfing me, the fakir was standing above me, laughing, and offering me a stone! The gall of it! To take away everything from me and give me a stone in return; my own stone, from my own land!"

"Ah!" cried Amir, who then became silent and wonderstruck at the happy coincidence of encountering the image he had heard in Baba's shabad through his master's dream.

"What does the stone mean?" Karoria asked gruffly.

---

[1] Lord.

"It is no ordinary stone, hazoor, but *the* stone, the philosopher's stone that turns iron into gold."

"What?" cried Karoria, sitting up in bed, his interest piquing at this bit of very important news, his imagination going wild with visions of untold wealth. "And where can I find it? Does he have it? Will he sell it? I'll let him have the land in return for it!" he cried magnanimously. Amir despaired for his master, but resolved to press forward with his explanation of the image.

"While I was at his *dera*,² Baba Nanak sang shabads that I recall vividly. In one of them he sang, 'Touching the philosopher's stone, metal is transformed into gold. Such is the glorious greatness of the society of saints.' The stone is a metaphor. God, hazoor, God is the philosopher's stone that turns darkness into light, suffering into joy, animals into humans, humans into angels, and death into life."

Karoria was disappointed at Amir's explanation, but knew in his heart that the stone he desired existed, and he was determined to find it when he felt better.

"Baba says," Amir continued, recalling how his dull and tarnished soul had sparkled as he listened to Baba's voice, "when one meets the Guru, what was turned to slag is again transformed into gold."

"Does this man call himself a guru?"

"He is a guru, hazoor, but Baba's finger always points to God, the Great Guru, not at himself; he says that God the Beloved alone is the Guru, the Guide who shows us the way. But those humans who cannot hear the Beloved calling to their souls need human gurus to guide them to the Adored One. I have tested him, and I know that Baba Nanak is my true guru. When I first arrived, Baba had just come from the fields, dressed unassumingly like a farmer, with a hoe on his shoulder."

"Plowing *my* land! Thief!"

"He put the hoe down and sat under a spreading banyan tree, where others were already waiting for him, including me. I was going to give him your message, hazoor, and tell him to vacate at once, and I was prepared to use force. But before I could do so, he wiped his sweaty brow and picked up a musical instrument and ran his fingers over the strings. Hazoor, I cannot describe to you what the sound did to me."

---

² Encampment, dwelling, hermitage.

Karoria's jealousy flared at the admiration in Amir's voice, and he shouted, "How dare you praise this man who is set on ruining me? Since he appeared, my retainers and soldiers have disobeyed my orders. Even my favorite horse has become a stubborn mule! I sent you there to evict him! What were you doing, listening to this magician's songs, you fool, you weakling?"

"When you hear even one strain of the song, the very first note, it casts a magic spell, for his words speak of marvelous things; the sound and the sense make your soul flutter its wings in the rib cage of your heart. Everything else falls away as you stand upon the revealed path before you, Baba's voice like an angel's, reminding you of higher things, of the journey you were born to make and which you have forgotten in the pursuit of other, ultimately trivial, things."

"And what was this song about?"

Amir shut his eyes to recall the sound and sense. He hummed a few notes haltingly, cleared his throat, and explained.

"I have been singing it to myself since my return and have memorized a few stanzas."

He sang the refrain, the sound of the first two syllables elongated as if out of time and touching infinity as they unfurled leisurely, making arabesques in the air before picking up the beat and completing the couplet as his hand gesticulated in accompaniment.

> Baba, maya saath na ho-ay.
> In maya jag mohia virla boojai ko-ay.

When Amir had sung a few stanzas and wound up the shabad, its lingering echo fading into silence, Karoria asked, "What does the song mean?"

"Any translation can only convey the shell of it, like the cocoon after the butterfly has flown. Translation can even kill it, hazoor. The ears have to hear the music, the words, and Baba's indescribable voice for the magic to happen. But the gist of it is, 'Brother, Maya will not aid you on this journey. She has bewitched the world. Only a few understand this.'"

"Amir, I did not know you could sing."

"You don't know a lot of things about me, hazoor. You don't know that something magical happened to me at the dera, and that I fell in love with

Guru Nanak and his message. I felt the kind of love I have felt for no one in my life, not my wife, not my many mistresses, not my children."

"Not even me?"

"Not even you."

"You are fired!" thundered Karoria.

Bowing his head, Amir began to back out of Karoria's bedroom.

"And I'm not going to give you that bonus I promised you!"

Amir left the room.

"Come back here!" Karoria shouted weakly, for the outburst had claimed his last bit of energy. It wasn't a command, but rather the cry of a child who felt suddenly very abandoned.

Amir returned.

"I have done nothing but accumulate wealth in your service, hazoor, but now my soul has heard a call it cannot refuse. Something wonderful has happened on the edges of your land. Infinity has opened up. Give up your tiny empire to live in the immensity of the universe! Do not feel threatened. Open wide your arms and embrace it! Such an opportunity will not come again."

Karoria's recent suffering had made him receptive to Amir Shah's advice. His bones aching, his blind rheumy eyes seeing only the webs of things, he yielded to an internal voice that prompted him to go. Slumped on Sohji, his thoughts vacillating between rage and hope, he began his journey to the edges of his land, to Baba. Several miles from Baba's camp, Sohji once again stood still and would not budge.

"Hazoor, get off your horse and go to Baba Nanak in all humility. Go on foot, master."

"But I am weak and feeble," Karoria said.

"You have no choice, hazoor. Your horse won't move. Pray to God for strength, and he will grant it."

Karoria alighted and promptly fell down. First he crawled on all fours, but as he neared the dera, his body was infused with strength, and he began to walk upright, feeling lighter and happier as he approached the hutment, his eyes gradually regaining sight as the sound of Baba's voice wafted to the ears of his soul.

Anik janam bichhurat dukh paaiaa
Kar geh layho pritam prabh raia.
(Separated from you, I have suffered for countless incarnations.
Take my hand, Beloved, my sovereign, my Lord!)

As Karoria stood there listening, the sound and the words pulled on his heartstrings, arousing him to shed the sickness of his imprisoned soul and live in a new, freer, and more joyous way. He collapsed at Baba's feet and clung to them as he sobbed like a baby.

"I give you all this land and more!" he cried.

Baba laughed loudly, gleefully, his bright laughter scattering light in every direction. Then, with twinkling eyes, he looked at Karoria in such a way that the rich man saw the land was not his to give, that everything belonged to God; that he could only be grateful to God for making him the instrument of this giving.

Karoria was humbled as the boundaries of his soul expanded. He had a vision of what his life could be in service to God and others, so he stayed at the dera for several weeks, shared meals with strangers, even poor and low-caste people, and listened to Baba's music and discourses. Karoria, full of new life, enthusiastically began to plan a city in the area, proportioning his land generously, giving orders, and laying the foundations of a temple, which Baba called *gurdwara*, the threshold of the Guru. Eagerly he ran to Baba and said, "We shall name this new city Nanakpur!"

Baba laughed and said, "But it is not mine. It belongs to the Creator who creates, gives, and takes away, to the One who gave it to you and now to my fellow Sikhs. Let us name this place Kartarpur, City of the Creator."

Baba's devotees, who now called themselves Sikhs, cleared land, built walls and houses of stone, fashioned plows and shares, prepared the soil, and planted vegetables, potatoes, corn, wheat, pulses, beans, and herbs; they built irrigation channels from the Ravi River, dug wells, and installed Persian wheels. They worked with zeal, love, and devotion, for after much suffering and struggle, a clear direction was revealed to them, a direction that gave energy to their bodies and peace and joy to their minds and hearts.

Baba, too, took off his traveling *chola*, dressed in ordinary farmer's clothes, and worked robustly, digging, plowing, and weeding with the others.

Baba wanted Kartarpur to be communal property where everyone had his or her residence, but Mardana changed all that. One day while Baba was surveying the land, Mardana arrived with the rabab on his shoulder and said to him, "Baba, I have always been obedient to you when you said 'Mardana, rabab chhaid, bani aee hai.' Now, I want you to play the rabab while I sing. Bani aee hai."

Baba smiled, took the rabab from him, and moved to sit under a nearby *kikar*[3] tree. Mardana started with the alaap of Raag Dhanasri. Baba closed his eyes and accompanied him, knowing full well what was coming. Mardana shut his eyes too and communed with God in a sweet, humble, unabashed and heart-to-heart way as he sang Saint Dhanna's[4] shabad.

> Gopaal tayraa aartaa
> jo jan tumree bhagat karantay
> tin kay kaaj savaarataa.
> (Lord, you who straighten out the lives of your devotees,
> this is my worship, this is my song;
> I beg you, give me the following things so that my mind
> and body are pleased and at peace.
> Make sure I have lentils, flour, and ghee; shoes, fine clothes, and grains of
> seven kinds, please; a milk cow, a water buffalo, a fine Turkish horse,
> and a good woman.
> Dhanna begs you humbly for these things, Lord.)

Baba sang along with feeling. It was a sight, the Saint and the Artist, sitting in the shade of a tree, asking God joyously, unabashedly, to provide for their creaturely needs and comforts.

"Baba," Mardana said, once an appropriate amount of time had elapsed after the singing. "I also want my very own piece of land, as large as you can make it, so that I can have an orchard, a vegetable garden, and a flower garden. I want to feel a sense of ownership, something I can bequeath to Fatima and my children. Please don't disappoint me now!"

---

[3] An Indian acacia tree.
[4] A medieval saint who lived in the 1400s and whose bani has been incorporated into the SGGS.

Mardana waited for a reply, ready for battle if it came to that.

"Yes, Mardana, let us pretend our land and homes belong to us as well as to the Creator," came the reply.

So everyone including Baba not only had his own portion of land, but also worked on a large tract of land held in common. The men and women labored in their own fields and devoted time to the common land, growing grain, lentils, and vegetables, which provided food to the common kitchen, called the *langar*, from which any visitor, from any religion or caste, could partake. People from other villages and towns donated giant skillets, pots, pans, and woks in which abundant food and halwa with pure ghee, wheat flour, and sugar were prepared. The halwa, called *kadaa parshad*, was always available to those who came to the temple.

Owners of kilns donated bricks and mortar with which small individual homes, communal buildings, and a temple were built. Word spread. More people thronged, bringing food and seeds, saplings and fruit trees, bulls and cattle.

When the foundations of the city were laid, all Baba's acquaintances and devotees came from far and wide to dig and carry. Sheikh Sajjan, the thug, came; the four thieves who tried to loot Baba came with their wives and children; Rai Bular, the enlightened ruler, now aged, who recognized the child Nanak as special, came; Nur Shah's girls came to collect herbs and cook for everyone; Kauda, much thinned, came; Muslim and Hindu scholars and fakirs came. Even Taakat, who after eons of being lost in the labyrinths of his mind became a human and a devotee of Guru Nanak, moved into Kartarpur with his family—but only after he had tested Baba with his fierce and searching mind. And of course, Karoria was a frequent visitor, and Sohji always galloped all the way to the dera.

Before they knew it, organically, easily, spontaneously, in *sahaja*, like a flower, Kartarpur began to grow, bloom, and flourish.

CHAPTER 19
Homecoming

Mardana sent several messengers to Fatima to tell her he was coming home. As he walked with long, eager strides, he imagined a
marvelous homecoming. Fatima would cook his favorite food: *kheer*,[1] *paranthas*,
saag,[2] and *makki de roti*,[3] and she would wear the *garaara*[4] she had worn on their
wedding, now faded and old, as a sign of her receptivity to him. Oh, he knew
she would have aged in the intervening years, but his mind stubbornly held on
to the image of her as young and beautiful. His children and grandchildren
would rush into his arms and adore him; his dog, Moti, would leap up on him
vigorously, almost knocking him down, and lick his face.

As he neared his home, Mardana saw an old woman at the door in dirty
clothes, uncombed grey hair flying in all directions. He knew she wasn't his
mother or Fatima's mother, for he had heard they were dead. Could Fatima
have hired a servant? Maybe Fatima was ill and this was the *daee*.[5] His heart
lurched with fear. No, he consoled himself, recalling that his aunt, Daulatan
Masi, lived with them now. It was probably her. The woman turned around.
He was about to ask her where Fatima was when he saw a familiar mole on

---

[1] Indian pudding made with rice, milk, sugar, and nuts.
[2] A Punjabi dish made with mustard leaves and ghee.
[3] A flat corn bread.
[4] An ankle-length split skirt worn by Muslim women.
[5] A nurse.

the woman's chin. It was Fatima—but oh, how ugly and old she had become! Not at all like the woman in his dreams! Her expression was cold, and when Mardana said her name, "Fatima," she just glared at him.

"Didn't you get the messages? I sent several that I was coming, and . . . I am home, and Baba is well, too," he rambled on as he walked through the courtyard littered with uncollected buffalo dung and chicken droppings, trying to cover up his disappointment and confusion. No smell of cooking food, no children, no grandchildren, no neighbors to greet the wandering minstrel with garlands of marigolds on his return.

Fatima turned around and went into the house without a word. Mardana followed her, his heart sinking: no peace at the end of his travels? No rewards for his holy life, no gain in devoting his life to a saint, who said devotion to saints brought the highest reward? Sorrowful and unhappy, he put his rabab and bag down in the usual place in the corner, by the unmade bed.

Daulatan Masi sat on a *manji* in a corner, looking at him intently, silently. He went to her and touched her feet. She giggled and withdrew them, then threw her arms around him and held on so tightly that Mardana had to disentangle himself with quite an effort. Something stirred and moved in a corner of the courtyard. An animal lay on a gunnysack, a dog, wagging his tail weakly. Mardana walked to him, his heart lurching with expectation: could it be? Yes, yes it was Moti, but oh, so aged and feeble! Mardana squatted down, and the dog licked his foot and looked at him with cloudy eyes, at once glad and mournful. Mardana picked him up and laid him in his lap, holding him close to his heart, tears streaming down his face as he sobbed in joy and sorrow, with all the heartbreak of a long-awaited but disappointing homecoming.

"Moti," he whispered. "My dear, dear friend, Moti!" Moti leaned into his body, licking his face feebly as he whimpered and yelped. After a long time of holding him, he put Moti down. In the courtyard, on the *thadaa*, which served as their bathing area, near a sheet tied with a string around it as a curtain for privacy, Mardana spied steam rising. A bucket of hot water for a bath! How his limbs ached. He walked over to it, and there by the bucket and the mug was the small, familiar, grimy clay bottle of mustard oil. He recalled how Fatima used to massage him, and then pour *lotas* of warm water on his hair as he soaped it. His heart began to well up with bitterness, but he heard Baba's voice in his head: *"Bina santokh naheen ko raajai."* (There is no satisfaction without contentment.) He calmed down and felt immensely grateful for the warm water and the bottle full of mustard oil. At least she had paid attention to this. He bathed, scrubbing off the dirt on his feet and hands with the pumice, and feeling the warmth of the water caressing his weary body. Later he poured the mustard oil into his cupped hand, rubbed his hands together, and applied it to his cracked feet and the rest of his body. It stung him, but he was grateful for it. His towel wrapped around him, he returned to his bed, his body ready for a rest.

He chuckled to himself, wondering what kind of reception Baba had received at the hands of his wife, Bibi Sulakhni. Perhaps her separation from Baba had softened her, but Mardana's imagination, swinging between images of Baba being chased around his courtyard by a wife with a rolling pin and a grand welcome, failed to fill in the lacunae of another's life.

Fatima could at least have made the bed, he thought. But he was so tired that upon lying down, he fell into a deep slumber almost instantly. His feverish brain dreamed of being chased by cannibals; of large chunks of gold that turned to ash in his hands; of Razaa, who turned into a hag before his eyes; of large cauldrons of food, so delicious-smelling; and of the sounds of children so delightful that they awoke him from sleep.

For a while, he couldn't tell where he was; but then reality stepped in. He opened the wooden chest that held his clothing. A clean but faded set of clothes lay on top. It was the set he had worn at his wedding and at every subsequent wedding in the family and neighborhood, the cloth thinned by many washings. As Mardana dressed, he realized that his dream of delicious-smelling food had been triggered by actuality. Fatima squatted by the *chulla*, placing cow-dung patties on the fire and blowing on them with the *phookhni*.[6] A large pot simmered and steamed on the fire, near which lay the *peedee*, the stringed stool she had made as part of her dowry for her wedding, and which she had repaired many times, tightening or replacing the strings. On stringed cots in the courtyard sat his family, waiting for him to awaken to greet him. Ah, it felt like a dream to Mardana; the kind of dream he'd had on his travels, imagining himself at home.

He walked out of the room and greeted his family members, whom he barely recognized. Many of them, like his daughter-in-law and grandchildren, were new to him. The meeting was awkward and shy. Silence reigned.

---

[6] A tube for blowing on fire.

Mardana sat down on the *peedee* that he knew was for him, and a grand-daughter came and sat shyly in his lap.

"My name is Aziza," she said. "And yours?"

"He's your Dadu Jaan,"[7] her mother scolded.

"Mardana," Mardana replied, thrilling at the sight of this lovely little creature, this being with his blood flowing through her veins.

"Dadu Jaan," she said, as if savoring the sounds of the new words. "Dadu Jaan, Dadu Jaan, Mardana. Mardana!"

All present burst into giggles and laughter, for a child never addressed the elders by their names but by the names of their roles in the family. The silence broke; everyone loosened up, relaxed, and began to chatter. Mardana heard about many little events of the family, news about his daughters who were married and residing in other towns, and rejoiced at finally being in the presence of loved ones.

Fatima placed a *thaali*[8] before Mardana—with not the politest of gestures and a little too loudly—and ladled, yes, *biryani*, with large chunks of goat meat and bones, lentils, vegetables, and fragrant rice. At first he resisted eating the meat, and then quietly, with gratitude to the goat, he sat and alternately fed his granddaughter and himself with his fingers. This soon became a mutual feeding, with Aziza putting some rice into his mouth with her tiny fingers.

Occasionally Fatima looked at him intently. As usual, she would wait till after he had finished partaking of the meal to begin hers. It was an old habit of hers to hold her own appetite in abeyance till those she had undertaken to feed had been fed. Mardana's eyes tried to catch hers, but she evaded them. He looked at her closely. She wasn't at all as young as he had fantasized she'd be, but she was still beautiful. Her hair was quite grey and her skin wasn't as taut and smooth as it once was, but it had a soft luminescence, a transparency, as if something was shining in and through her.

When the meal was over, Fatima and his daughter-in-law scrubbed the pots with ashes from the fire. Later, after she had bathed, Fatima came to their bed wearing the dear familiar dress of his dreams. Mardana's heart swelled with love. He held open his arms and she moved toward him, but instead of

---

[7] *Dadu* is an affectionate variation of "dada" or "grandfather," and *Jaan* means "my life," an affectionate endearment.

[8] An Indian plate, bigger than the Western one, large enough to hold small bowls containing different curries, lentils, and yogurt, as well as *rotis* and rice.

letting him hold her, she beat his chest with her fists, crying and weeping and sobbing and cursing him for being gone from home for so very long. He didn't try to defend himself, but just let her sob and talk. How many things she said, some very hurtful, some very pleading. After she expressed her rage, hurt, and feelings of abandonment, she calmed down, and turned to him in love and softness. And though their union was far gentler than in their youth and in Mardana's fantasies, Allah was still present.

PART II

Seeds

CHAPTER 20
Shehzada

Mardana sat on his comfortable bed in Kartarpur, watching Shehzada, his son, eating in the corner of the room that served both as a bedroom and kitchen in the winter. Shehzada appeared to be in a hurry. He was tearing the *rotis* apart, scooping up large amounts of *sabzi*[1] and *daal* with them, stuffing them in his cheek pouches, and chewing furiously as his hands prepared the next mouthful. There seemed to be an urgency to his eating, a fear that the plate might vanish before his eyes at any moment.

He hasn't even eaten a mouthful before he's grabbing for more, Mardana thought. *I too have been gluttonous, but Baba has taught me that Allah always provides. Who will teach my son, who doesn't listen to me and refuses to visit Baba, let alone accompany him on the rabab? How many generations will keep stumbling before they finally learn? But wisdom cannot be passed on to the generations, for the journey is new with each person. Each must learn through his mistakes. Yet I should guide him a little at least, like Baba guided me.*

"Slow down," Mardana said to him. But the young man only glowered at him, his eyes catching a gleam from the cooking fire and lighting up like an animal's, uncomprehending and mistrusting.

Shehzada choked on his food and began to cough.

"Slow down," Mardana said again.

---

[1] Curried vegetables.

This time Shehzada growled with his mouth full of food, "Who are you to tell me?"

I'm your father! Mardana wanted to yell, but bit his tongue, confused and angry at the way his son had turned out in his absence. He heard Baba's voice in his head, advising him to speak sweetly.

"Just an old man who wants to be listened to and loved, my son."

"Where were you when I wanted to be listened to and loved?" Shehzada barked, getting up, plate in hand, and leaving the room.

Mardana sighed. *Sons!* Baba was having trouble with his as well. They hadn't come to Kartarpur when Baba had sent for them and his wife, Sulakhni. The older son, Sri Chand, revolting against his father's path of engagement with the world in all its aspects, had become an *udasi*, an ascetic, with long, matted hair and a body smeared with ashes from the crematorium, practicing celibacy and severe austerities. His younger son, Lakhmi Das, had become an angry young man who found relief in hunting wild animals mercilessly. When Lakhmi Das finally moved to Kartarpur—lured no doubt by the forests teeming with wild animals around the new township, and the hope of inheriting his father's well-established and lucrative commune—Mardana had witnessed many angry scenes between son and father. Lakhmi Das refused to work in the fields, drank wine and other liquors, woke up late, and did not participate in or contribute to the life of the community.

Sons! Mardana thought again, sliding down further in his bed next to Aziza, who was sleeping after intense play, till he was supine. He had thought he would finally be happy once he got home. He was, for the most part, but every circumstance of one's life has its conflicts and its sorrows, he reasoned. He was glad he didn't have to forage for food, but his stomach bothered him often; he was glad for his wife's presence in his bed, but she was often distant, or nagged him. His one unalloyed joy was his granddaughter, Aziza. She was his constant companion, going with him to the dera, orchard, garden, and fields, often strumming his rabab in a childlike way, snuggling up with him in his bed, and listening with attention and delight to his tales. Spontaneously, without any effort or even intention, he began to teach her how to hold the rabab and bow, where to place her fingers, the alphabet of music. He began with simple, fundamental notes, the *sa*, then moved on to how to string it with another note, and then another, to make a necklace of sounds.

How dear she is! he thought, looking at her sleeping, innocent face and feeling a strong tug in his chest as his heartstrings vibrated with love.

Mulling over his new life, Mardana pulled the blanket up to his chin. Through the open door he could see Fatima at her wheel, spinning cloth in a very self-absorbed way. There was a part of her that didn't belong to him anymore. Mardana wondered if it ever had. She herself had said many times to him since his return that she had been alone so long she had learned to enjoy her precious solitude, that there was no going back now. The thought pained Mardana, for now, more than ever, he wanted to clasp her to his heart, lean on and depend upon her. Each time he did, Fatima behaved in a manner that severed the tentacles of his attachment. Once, when Mardana had tried to change something about the functioning of the household, she had said, "I'm doing it, and this is how I do it. Like it or not." She didn't hesitate to tell him what was in her heart, or scold him when she felt she needed to. The other day she said, "What right have you to scold or be harsh with Shehzada? Where were you when he was growing up? Who did he have to discipline him, to show him the way?"

They had fought continuously since his return and since the family's move to their new home in Kartarpur. It was a fight to even get her to move from Talwandi, where she had lived in his absence. No, not all was well since his return. He recited one of Baba's lines from a long song called *aasaa di var*, the Song of Hope—or rather, the War for Hope—that Baba had composed since his return, and which Mardana had sung along with him while accompanying him on the rabab.

Koorh meeaan, koorh bibi, khap hoai khaar.
(All relationships are garbage when we forget
our relationship with the Creator.)

I have to remember to love Fatima as a spark of God, Mardana mulled. He took a deep breath and returned to his quiet center, the place where there was no separation between Allah and himself. *When that connection is primary, all other relationships fall into place. When it isn't, attachment ruins love. Ah, but we are human and forgetting and falling from grace is our destiny.*

Looking across the courtyard and seeing Fatima's self-absorbed face as she worked at her loom, Mardana thought, *I do love her. When we are in harmony, what bliss!*

Mardana's thought, traveling through the plasma of space, found its mark. Fatima looked up at him lazing on the bed, and smiled. He smiled back, warmth suffusing his heart.

What a woman! She scolds me and feeds me halwa. She even likes her new home; I can tell she loves roaming around in the orchard and garden before dawn, plucking vegetables and fruit. She likes the two sheep I bought for her; she enjoys taking them out to graze in the surrounding forests, fleecing them, and spinning the yarn. Mardana ran his fingers over the soft, warm *loee* that Fatima had woven for him, which he wore on cold mornings and evenings and took with him when he sang and played before the congregation.

Mardana was grateful that God had fulfilled all of his desires. He wished again that Fatima was more obedient, but she did take good care of the home and family. The congregation was generous and always donated money to him, heaping it before his feet as he accompanied Baba in the morning and evening prayers, and the fields of Kartarpur, fertile with rich soil and fruit trees, yielded abundance. There was no shortage of food, and though he didn't have a Turkish horse, he had a water buffalo that gave ample milk for his favorite things, butter, ghee, *kheer,* and *barfi,* and he had two bulls to plow his fields and pull the cart.

"Thank you, God, thank you, thank you, thank you," Mardana prayed, sliding further under the quilt. "There's only one other thing. Put some sense into Shehzada's head so he agrees to become Baba's rababi, and I can retire."

Immediately after his request, Mardana paused. *No, this was not the way to pray,* he thought, remembering a time of wandering lost in the mazes of his desires when his prayers for a more obedient mate had led him to death's door. He amended his prayer: "I would like Shehzada to accompany Baba, but if you know it is not in my interest to get this wish, please help me accept your choice for me."

Mardana wondered vaguely whether he should sit up and meditate, but his body had its own agenda. He consoled himself with Baba's phrase: "Tan mein manua man mein sacha." (Keep your mind in your body and the True One in your mind.)

"My mind and body just want to rest," he admitted to himself.

Mardana's thoughts turned to Baba. Ten years younger than Mardana, Baba was actively engaged in all aspects of his new life, including feeding the bodies, minds, and souls of his congregation. While younger men did the heavy labor of plowing and preparing the fields, Baba often sowed the seeds, casting them far and wide, and joined the men and women in irrigating, weeding, composting, and harvesting. He worked in the kitchen, too, helping prepare food in the langar, and cleaning utensils. Baba did not shy away from any task. In addition, he was composing spiritual epics for each of the seasons.

As he lay on his bed, Mardana's thoughts began to lose focus and melted into a warm, comforting soup of unconsciousness as he drifted toward slumber, which was happily interrupted by Aziza waking and saying, "Dadu Jaan Mardana, tell me another story!"

Mardana obliged. When Fatima came into the room, sat on a *peedee*, and began to spin as she listened to his tale, Mardana's happiness was complete.

CHAPTER 21
In His Orchard

Watching the beauty of the dawn, the bands of pink and blue on the horizon as the darkness imperceptibly brightened into day, and listening to the sounds of birds chirping and his granddaughter's early-morning prattling, Mardana knew he was going to spend the day in his garden. The sun was shining outside, and though there was a chill in the air, the sunlight was warm and welcoming. Wrapping his warm *loee* tightly around his shoulders, Mardana walked out of his room, through the court-yard, and into the plot of land behind his house that served as an orchard, vegetable patch, and flower garden.

Mardana sat a while to warm his bones in a sunny spot of land facing south. He had placed a *manji* here to rest on. This was his favorite spot out-doors, a place to rest from his labors and let his mind wander hither and thither in time, review his days, take stock of his present and past life, and linger and reminisce from a vantage point looking down upon the moving, ever-diminishing arc of his life. Far less remained than had unfolded, and yet he felt his life had dilated somehow to include a bit of eternity.

He looked at his garden, his own little piece of the world, at the thick-ening trunks of his guava and mango trees, the crisp leaves luminous against the deep blue sky of the morning, the tender stalks of mustard, the blooming roots of winter tubers and herbs, and the pink and yellow roses, with a deep sense of satisfaction and well-being. He felt a sensation of lightness, a little leap of joy within his heart that signaled sheer delight at being.

How deeply fulfilled he felt, how appreciative of the small pleasures and comforts of the ordinary life: his morning ritual of drinking herbal teas, sitting with Fatima in silence, and going to the dera when he felt like it—not out of duty, but to enjoy the *rawnak*, the ongoing festive atmosphere, and to listen to Baba singing as Shehzada accompanied him.

"It was the money!" Mardana chuckled, thinking back on the day Shehzada came to him and said, "Okay, I will take over from you." He had seen how many coins the congregation heaped before Mardana as he played, how deeply loved, respected, and admired his father was, not only in the dera, but far and wide. "He hasn't given up any of his ambitions, but it suits him for now to do this. He will grow from this experience and learn how much more valuable than money and fame are the gifts Baba has to bestow!"

Mardana gave thanks for this development. He had taken several years to recuperate from his travels, to learn to listen to his aging body's tempo and to live in tune with its rhythms without overtaxing it in any way. He didn't mind that others, sometimes even Fatima, called him lazy for not wanting to graze the sheep or get fodder for the cow. Sometimes he did help her, or hired help, but his conviction that he had earned the right to be lazy was absolute and unwavering. What others termed lazy he called living consciously, observing the internal weather of his soul, adjusting his activities accordingly, riding his body's energy waves, nurturing the vessel that had been through many hardships during his journeys and had mutely endured them, like a stubborn but loyal donkey. Now he listened when his body spoke, applied balm to its aching joints and sore muscles, collected herbs that Fatima suggested for his digestion and other ailments, and took the time to brew them correctly.

Mardana looked down at his body, at the slight paunch that he deemed a sign of prosperity, at his still-skinny legs in socks and sandals that had walked halfway across the world and back, and said aloud, "My body is my idol."

Startled and disturbed at the thought, Mardana wondered if he was blaspheming. He stood under the guava tree, and one of Baba's shabads swam into his memory, which he began to hum. *The body is God's temple through which He experiences his own creation.*

Mardana stood still as the words sprang alive in his consciousness. He understood that it did not mean "I am God," for he had become humble enough to know this smacked of pride, but rather that he was a part of the pulsing, thrusting, and procreating energy of the universe, for which the human word was God. All the knowledge in his head descended into his body and soul and pulsed with life. This was no mere thought, but experience.

Mardana saw a guava on the tree. Midway between dark green and yellow, half raw and half ripe, it was just the way he liked it. He reached up and touched it; it fell into his hand, ready to be eaten. After rubbing it on his clothes, he bit into its crunchy sweetness.

This has to be savored sitting down, he thought, making himself comfortable on the sunny *manji* again. Looking lovingly at the fruit in his hand, then biting into it and spitting out the hard seeds, Mardana admitted to himself that he adored and worshipped his body.

"So treat it like you would treat an idol. Love it, tend it, don't scold or torture it with unrealistic desires and disturbing thoughts. Do I have any unrealistic desires and disturbing thoughts?" he asked himself. He had to admit his ambitions and desires were far worldlier than his lot. He had wanted to be a world-renowned artist, singer, and rababi. This old longing darkened his inner landscape and made him aware of the restless phantoms still lurking in his consciousness. As he went about doing his chores in the garden, chaos began to gather in his brain and poisoned his joy. "Stop it, Mardana. Stop thinking thoughts that make you unhappy! Conquer your mind; have more control over it!" he said aloud as he took his scissors and cut off dead heads on the rosebush.

Mardana took a deep breath, calming himself.

Everything I feel and think is God. Even doubt and all the thoughts that question, disbelieve, and mistrust God are God's, Mardana thought. He knew this truth was a relative one and did not apply to those feelings and thoughts he knew he had to take responsibility for. This insight made Mardana pause in his labors in jubilation, joy radiating in concentric circles around his heart, immense spaces unfurling in his mind and soul.

Disbelief and mistrust arise when our vision of God is a projection of our own smallness, which can't comprehend and envision His immense mystery.

You are an ocean and I am just a tiny fish—how can I know your limits? Mardana hummed Baba's words as he went about pruning and weeding.

Because Mardana had come to the Divine after a lot of exploration and rebellion, he now tethered himself to God securely, albeit with a long and winding leash. Contrasted with his self-conscious attempts at reaching God in the goat pen, this attachment was an entirely voluntary and conscious act; it was something he chose to do. He loved the magic that God made in his life.

No, he thought, putting cured buffalo dung in a basket and taking it to the roses. *It is not a choice but a given, something I was born with and can't avoid, like destiny. These are the terms of my existence. I have to willingly choose the given, to walk the path laid before me. After a lifetime, a moon has arisen in the sky of my soul that illumines my darkness. Baba is this moon.*

Mardana began singing Baba's spring song.

> In all ten directions, the branches are green and alive.
> That which ripens slowly is sweet.

"I am blooming," he said aloud, digging around the roots of the trees and feeding them dung. "I have bloomed into this joy easily, in *sahaja*, naturally, in the course of things, like this fruit-bearing tree: nothing forced, with no interference and struggling on my part. This gift is *prasad*,[1] the sweetest of halwa."

For several hours, Mardana worked in his garden, fully engaged, with not a thought in his head or feeling in his heart, till he became aware of his aches and pains and moved indoors to lie down for a little rest.

---

[1] Indian pudding made with flour, ghee, and sugar, given as a blessing to devotees who visit the temple.

CHAPTER 22
At the Dera

Removing his shoes before getting into bed, ready to have a nice midday nap after his labors in the garden, Mardana had a disturbing thought. *Everything that blooms dies!*

This thought became a pulsing sensation in his aging heart, which he clutched instinctively in fear.

Many images attended this sensation—petals falling, rotten fruit, dead leaves and limbs, and above all, the memory of Moti lying dead in the courtyard the morning after he had arrived home from his journeys. Mardana had gone to feed him and called, "Moti, Moti!" but he didn't respond. Mardana had thought he was sleeping blissfully, but when he came closer he saw there was no breath in him, and he was limp and unmoving.

The dread Mardana felt arose from a visceral certainty of his own demise, a final good-bye to everything he had felt and known. Never again would he wear shoes as he got out of bed; never again would he be able to get up at all. He would be carried, like Moti was carried, and placed in a pit in the earth.

Mardana called out to Fatima, even though he knew she was out with her friends, grazing her sheep. He felt himself getting angry with her for being so self-absorbed.

"Calm down, Mardana, calm down," he said to himself, as to a child, recalling images of Fatima's growing attachment to him. Just the night before, when he had woken from a nightmare of being in a tiny boat on the ocean at night, he had turned to her, and she had held and stroked him back to sleep. The memory of it calmed him down a bit, but his physical agitation remained. He wanted to call out to someone, anyone, but no one was around. Shehzada was on his way to the dera for evening prayers; even the children were out playing. He lay down with the hope that the feeling would pass, but he only flailed about under the quilt, his agitation increasing multifold. He knew he had to do something, so he got out of bed and headed toward the dera.

He was considerably cheered when his granddaughter ran after him from behind, crying "Dadu Jaan! Dadu Jaan!" She held his hand and skipped along with him, chattering away.

Mardana walked into a busy, bustling scene that immediately alleviated his fear of an imminent end. Lakhmi Das, Baba's younger son who never attended the singing sessions, was on his horse, going off to hunt with a retinue of dogs and companions; a group of women, including Bibi Sulakhni, were milking cows and chatting merrily, some churning milk to make butter and butter-milk; children were playing ball in a field, and Baba, still looking muscular and strong, was playing along with them to much laughter and jollity; dogs and puppies, lambs and calves and mares were barking, bleating, and neighing; yoked bullocks, some dragging plowshares, others pulling carts with baskets laden with fruit, vegetables, corn, and sugarcane, were coming in from the fields; women were cooking on colossal skillets and cauldrons for the evening langar; strong young men and women were feeding a roaring fire beneath a giant wok, while others were stirring steaming cane juice to boil it down into a thickened paste of brown sugar, later to be made into lumps for storage in earthenware vats; and a nawab in silks, attended by his many well-dressed servants, was arguing with a young man.

"I have donated money! I don't want to eat with everyone; I want to eat with the guru!"

"I'm sorry, sahib, we all eat together, no matter what station of life we belong to. Even the guru and his family eat at the langar."

Mardana walked past these scenes, greeted by people who bowed to him and touched his feet reverentially. He walked past Mata Tripta, Baba's mother, sitting on a *peedee*, supervising the langar, who smiled at Mardana as he bowed to her, as did Mehta Kallu, absently and distantly, walking with his hands locked behind him, dressed well and looking thoughtful, satisfied, and much softened by age. Mardana could guess what he was thinking, playing a mono-logue in his head about Mehta's state of mind: *"This no-good son of mine has done well. I had such high hopes of him when he was born. With his popularity with Rai Bular and Daulat Khan, he could have become powerful in the world, a lord, with buggies and horses and fine clothes. I always wanted that, wanted him to fulfill my desires for him. But he has not done badly in this God business. There must be something to him if so many people follow and love him. And I am grateful he called us to Kartarpur in our old age. This is a comfortable life, and his devotees take such good care of us."*

Mardana took off his shoes and walked into the gurdwara at the center of the dera. Shehzada was already there, joking with a youthful *tabla* player. Mardana felt a pang at the sight; why didn't his son smile and laugh with him that way? He felt a twinge of sadness as son and father acknowledged each other without saying a word. Aziza ran to the rabab by her father and started to strum it. Shehzada took it away from her and she began to cry till a young boy, about eight or nine years old, came into the gurdwara with a broom in his hand. She ran to him and they tussled over the broom. The boy got her another broom, and they both swept the floor exuberantly. Mardana couldn't take his eyes off the radiant and healthy face of the young boy.

"Who is he?" Mardana turned to Shehzada.

"I don't know," the *tabla* player replied, "but he's in the dera a lot, working in the fields or the langar, going wherever an extra hand is needed, and falling asleep wherever he gets tired. Yesterday he fell asleep driving the bullock cart! But the bulls knew where to go and came right here. He's here for morning and evening kirtan, sits cross-legged, shuts his eyes, and sways to the music like a cobra to the vibrations of a flute."

Men, women, and children of all ages began pouring into the gurdwara as Mardana watched, looking mainly at the younger people, admiring and envying them their youth. *Like little sprouting seeds in the garden,* he thought. Baba, carrying his grandson, Dharam Chand, walked in looking healthy and vigorous from daily physical labor, wearing a loose turban and a *kurta pajama,*[1] his beard turning silver and long. He greeted everyone cheerfully, individually, by name. It was the hour before the evening singing of prayers, the hour when people from the community came to discuss their concerns with Baba in an informal way.

---

[1] A long shirt and pajamas worn by men.

The young boy genuflected before Baba, lying down full length before standing up and resuming his task of sweeping. Baba sat near Mardana, lovingly touching him on the shoulder.

"Who is that young boy?" Mardana asked Baba.

"I want to know, too. He has been coming regularly for many days now. Boy, come here!"

The boy came running and touched Baba's feet.

"What's your name? Where do you come from?"

"Taru Poppat," the boy replied. "I come here from the next village to graze my cows and goats."

"You are too young to spend all your time at the dera. You should be sleeping, eating, studying, and playing. Go, do what other children do!" Baba said.

The boy stood up, his face quavering on the verge of tears, and said defiantly, "No, I won't go!"

"Obey the guru, you fool!" A woman from the congregation said.

"I won't!" the boy cried.

"Baba Nanak values obedience highly. Go if he says go."

"I always do what I am told, don't I?"

"Except now," the woman said. "Obedience to a guru is a very important quality! How else will you learn humility and obedience to God's will?"

"But this is not God's will, but Baba's, and Baba can change his mind about his order."

The congregation burst into laughter.

"It wasn't an order, child, just a suggestion," Baba said.

"All the more reason for me not to obey a suggestion. When anyone tells me to do anything I don't refuse."

"It's true," someone said.

"Tell me, Taru, why do you come to the dera every day?"

Taru Poppat took a long breath and explained.

"Many things happened in the last few months, Baba Jee. First, some Muslim soldiers allowed their horses to eat up all of our sprouting grains. Second, my mother sends me out to graze our two buffalo every day and to collect wood. Together with big pieces of wood I collect, I also gather small ones, twigs and things. One day I sat by my mother as she lit the fire, and I saw her put the small pieces under and around the large ones, and I asked her why she did that. 'The small ones catch fire first,' she said, and as I watched I saw the twigs catch fire right away, burn brightly, lighting the bigger ones, then turning to ash. I have been thinking: since I am small, like sprouting grain, like a small twig, I could burn up and die any time, and I should shine brightly before that happens."

The audience was stunned into silence by the words of one so young. Mardana realized that his attraction to the boy was no ordinary attraction, but something profound. As the boy spoke, he felt a warm sensation in the region of his heart. The leap of worry about the sensation being fatal was almost instantly smothered by a flame of love so powerful that he sat in total stillness, fully alert and attentive to the goings-on inside his body and brain. The boy's presence and words had fanned an ember within his heart, long smoldering beneath a pile of worldly desires. His hands instinctively flew up and cupped his breast in a gesture of protection for the flame. Whatever remained of his life, his task henceforth was to protect and fan this fragile flame till it became a conflagration in which he perished.

"And if I can die any time, I better find out what it is I am here to do, so I can do it, I thought," Taru Poppat continued.

"And have you found out what you are here to do, Taru?"

"To catch the fire of love for God and his whole creation, all humans, animals, plants, everything beautiful and ugly, living and not living, for as you say, every grain of dirt and stone is alive with God, Baba Jee."

"So, you know what you are here to do. Why come here every day? You can do that anywhere."

"I'm here to learn how to do it. Also, I am afraid of dying. Can you help me, Baba Jee?"

"You don't need me, Taru; the Guide has already taken your hand and set you on the path. You have already caught fire. When it is your time to die, death, which the world so fears, will be peaceful and joyous, like your wedding day, when you change out of the cloth of your body and move naked into your Beloved's embrace."

Baba shut his eyes and was silent a long time while the congregation sat, amazed and grateful for witnessing such a magical moment. When Baba opened his eyes he looked at Taru and said, "But you will not die young, Taru; you will have a long, long life. From now on we will call you Buddha Jee, the Ancient One."

Taru started to skip around, shouting, "I am Buddha Jee! I am Buddha Jee!"

A man, impressed by how the child had so simplified Baba's teaching, asked him: "What else have you learned from Baba Jee?"

"God is our breath, and our breath is the string on which the moments of our lives are strung. I have learned to remember this with each breath. I want to be like Baba, like the *chatrik*[2] bird whose thirst is not quenched with any drop of water, but *amrit*. Without this elixir, all our wanting only leaves us thirstier."

The audience, marveling at the phenomenon of this young but old child, was silent a long time before a woman broke the silence.

---

[2] A mythic bird who only drinks ambrosia.

"Baba, I don't understand how we should love but stay detached. How can we love without attachment?"

Baba, as was his custom when a question was asked, looked to the congregation to see if any gurmukh wanted to answer it.

"Attachment happens when we think the people we love belong to us instead of the Creator," another woman replied softly. Everyone knew she was the woman who had lost a young child to illness not too long ago. "When there is worry and pulling, fear and struggle in a relationship, when we want to control the outcome of something, there is attachment. Love them, take care of them the best you know how, but don't hold on to them with ropes of what you think is love. When we clutch too tightly, we do not love, but fear; and fear keeps us from love. I have learned I can't clutch even my own life too tightly, that I must be ready to sacrifice it to God when he asks for it."

Mardana's awareness, heightened by his encounter with his own demise, stood at attention and drank in all the words. Readiness was the key. *I have lived in a pen my whole life,* he thought, *doing mein, mein, mein.*[3] *From now on I will do tuun, tuun, tuun.*[4]

Baba smiled lovingly at the woman, and the congregation knew the answer had his assent.

"Baba Jee, I have been praying to God to straighten out some of my relationships, but God hasn't obliged," a man asked.

"Don't pray to get this or that, but pray for the strength to accept God's ways. God wants some relationships to be conflicted, like husbands and wives . . . "

The congregation laughed.

"And fathers and sons." Baba and the congregation were quiet. Baba's conflicted relationship with his sons was an open secret. "And we have to accept the conflict, too, and bear it calmly when it cannot be resolved."

"Baba Jee, I don't understand this business about contentment. You say that without contentment our hungers cannot be satisfied, but there would be no progress if we were all content."

"I think contentment and gratitude go hand in hand," someone said. "I think what Baba means is to be content with every condition of every moment; with everything that is. This is true submission and true freedom all at once.

---

[3] Me, me, me. Also echoes the bleating of a goat.
[4] You, you, you.

And sometimes we are discontent with what is, and have the desire to change it. We have to be content with this desire, too."

"Baba, how can we be content with all the evil in the world? How can brutal murders, rapes, crimes, and cruelty against children be God's will?"

"We cannot understand God's ways. We have to speak out and do what we can against cruelty and injustice. We have to live like warriors. And a gurmukh is always aware of the shadows in his own heart."

"What is the difference between a manmukh and a gurmukh?" someone asked.

"The ego is the center of a manmukh's life," Baba said. "He can't see past his little span of one life; he clings to his current physical life, curses God and the universe, and dies having squandered the gift of consciousness. The gurmukh doesn't fear death, because he has surrendered his ego to God long before his death and has made the larger life—God's people, creation, nature, and the universe—his center. He knows he is only a part of a vaster whole and that he contains this infinity in the center of his being. The gurmukh has a profound acceptance of what is. Death and the Beloved are his constant companions, heightening his consciousness of himself and his life. When he dies he becomes one with his Beloved, gets off the wheel of *samsara*,[5] and does not reincarnate."

After the silence that always followed Baba's words, a man asked, "Baba, what if you want to incarnate? What if you love life so much that you want to come back?"

"Then make sure you earn good karma, so you can come back and enjoy all the delights and pleasures of this life," Baba said.

"Baba, I have a lot of the qualities of a manmukh," a woman said.

"We are all manmukhs who have to learn to become gurmukhs," Baba said.

"Even you, Baba?"

Baba was silent. Shehzada, already sensitive to Baba's moods, began to tune the rabab. Baba sang:

"My demerits cannot be counted. I wandered through countless lifetimes without finding shelter anywhere. I took the form of many plants and trees and animals, was born into the families of snakes and flying birds. I broke into the shops of the city and well-guarded palaces, stole from them, then

---

[5] The wheel or cycle of life that extends over many lifetimes and incarnations.

snuck home to hide what I had stolen. I looked behind me to see no one was following me; but how could I hide from my Beloved? Entangled in Maya's web, attached to people and ideas and my own self-will, anxious, worried, and crying out in pain and agony, I roamed about blindly. As the seas and the oceans are overflowing with water, so vast are my sins. I was born foolish and ignorant, but I found sanctuary in the Loved One's embrace."

Baba's words shocked some in the audience. Those needing to believe in and follow a perfect, flawless god, or at least a superhuman, were disappointed; others took heart that if such a being as Baba could admit this, there was hope that they too could awaken into the larger life. Mardana knew, from having played along and sung with him, how often Baba had cried out to God from the depths of his soul, how totally human he was in his response to life, in his suffering. It was this humanity that made Baba so humble and compassionate. It was this, too, that fueled his inspiration for music and song, which was the Path, paved with notes and words, on which he flew into the Beloved's embrace. Mardana knew this because he had experienced this flight when he sang with Baba, when they both became one string vibrating to God's animating touch.

When Baba finished singing, a man from the congregation asked, "Is everything destiny, or do we have free choice?"

Before Baba could answer the question, Gareeb Mal, with a bloody bandage tied to his foot, limped into the temple, accompanied by his brother, Baldev. While Gareeb Mal prostrated himself before the guru, placing a handful of berries before him as an offering, Baldev stood aloof. Everyone at the dera knew that Baldev and Gareeb, residents of a nearby village, were opposites in appearance and nature. Gareeb, in bare feet, torn clothes, and a grubby turban, worked daily in the dera, cooking and serving food to the congregation, washing utensils with ash, sweeping and cleaning the compound, sitting devotedly at the feet of his guru, contemplating his words and listening to his kirtan; Baldev, dapper and well-dressed with a feather in his cap, was a criminal who attacked caravans, looted travelers, stole grain and goods, and brazenly cheated whomever he could.

The congregation turned eagerly toward these two, knowing a drama was about to unfold.

CHAPTER 23
Ashes and Gold

"Brother Baldev, what brings you here today?" Baba called out to him cheerfully.

"Come on, Gareeb, ask him," Baldev said with a smirk on his face. "I don't have all day for this."

"Guru Jee," Gareeb Mal spoke, standing before Baba with folded hands, "Baldev says I get nothing but bad luck in serving you."

"Does he? And what do you think, Gareeb?"

"I don't know what to think, Guru Jee. That's why I'm here. You see, I ran into Baldev at the crossroads, and he asked me, 'Why the bandage on the foot?' I explained that I had stepped on a large thorn that pierced my foot as I was picking berries for you, Guru Jee. He laughed at me and said, 'You poor thing! Are these the rewards you get for being such a good man? You live in a shack, your clothes are torn, you're skinny and starved, and now you get badly injured by a thorn while picking berries for your guru, while I, your bad brother, find a gold coin.'"

Baldev took a gold coin from his shirt pocket and held it up for the congregation to see.

"If only I had found the coin! I thought, filled with longing. What couldn't I do with it? Patch my leaking roof, buy some clothes for my wife, a pair of shoes for my little one who has outgrown her old pair and is now walking in bare feet. 'Where did you get this?' I asked him," Gareeb said, continuing his story. "'The entire village is talking about your exploits yesterday. Did you loot a prince? Baldev, Baldev,' I said, 'When will you give up your evil ways?'"

"Stop rambling and get to the point!" Baldev shouted rudely.

"But the point is a long one. I have to tell Guru Jee how the whole thing unfolded. Baldev said to me—"

"I'll tell them what I said to you," Baldev said. "Everyone is always giving me lectures about giving up my ways. Why should I give up my ways? Instead, he should convert to my ways. There are a lot of advantages to it. It pays, for one. Look at him. For all his goodness, he is punished by a thorn in his foot, while I am rewarded by the universe," Baldev said, tossing the gold coin in the air.

"Do you have an explanation for that?" Baldev said, looking at Baba in a very insolent way.

"Let me see the coin," Baba said, extending his hand, and Baldev put the coin on Nanak's palm. Baba looked at it closely, rubbed it on his robe, and then returned it to Baldev.

"That's exactly what he said, Baba Jee, and just like that: 'Do you have an explanation for that?' 'No,' I replied. A dark cloud of doubt drifted through my mind as I wondered if Baldev was right. Sometimes the only food I eat is the food I get here at the langar, Guru Jee; in the winters my family and I are often cold. My life is not exactly joyous, either. Sometimes life feels like a penance. And I thought, perhaps I shouldn't come to the dera anymore. Maybe I shouldn't listen to all that talk about not having an ego and eating what you are given. It is the people with egos who get all the good luck."

"Baba has never said we shouldn't have an ego; that's just your interpretation of it," a youth from the congregation spoke up. "Baba says we are born in ego and die in ego. It is by the ego that we are either foolish or wise. You need an ego to live, but the ego must bow before the Guide."

"But I also thought, perhaps this business of hukum, of obeying the will of God, is what keeps me away from my destiny. It doesn't get me anywhere in life. I feel hopeless, Guru Jee, and when I said to Baldev, 'Let's go to Baba and see if he has an explanation,' he laughed and said, 'He's just going to give you some mystical rigmarole, some spiritual opium, to quell your doubts.'" Gareeb concluded his story and looked hopefully at Guru Nanak.

"Oh Gareeb, give thanks for your good luck today!" Baba said.

"Good luck, Baba Jee?" Gareeb asked.

"Yes, give alms for the thorn in your foot! In your past life you lived like Baldev: following your will, plundering and looting and harming your fellow brothers and sisters. You had wealth and success, but no awareness, no wonder at the great mystery of life, no gratitude for the gift of consciousness. Your karma was so bad, Gareeb, that by its infallible and unavoidable law, you were meant to hang today. But by choosing the right path in this life, you have atoned and mitigated that sentence to a thorn in your foot."

"Baba, your explanation cannot be proved. Who knows whether there is karma or reincarnation?" Baldev said. "A thorn in the foot is a thorn in the foot, and a gold coin is a gold coin. Gareeb got hurt today, and I was rewarded. No one can change that!"

"And you, Baldev, lament your misfortune!" Baba Nanak said, turning to Baldev.

"Misfortune?" Baldev laughed, holding up the coin that shone rather brightly after Baba had rubbed it on his robe.

"You were a good man in your past life, Baldev, thinking of others, kind and generous, grateful for whatever little you had. But on your deathbed you had the same thoughts that Gareeb is having today and resolved in your next life to live for yourself alone and grab whatever you could for your own welfare at the cost of others' lives, limbs, or peace of mind. Because of your good karma in your past life, you were going to get a big pot full of gold today. But by your choices and actions in this life, you have turned all but this one coin to ash."

Baldev's ears pricked up at Baba's last word.

"Ash?"

"Yes, ash, Baldev."

"How . . . how did you . . . know?" Baldev spluttered. "This coin was sitting on top of a jar full of ashes! As I was squatting in the fields, a buried earthenware rim caught my attention. I dug it out; it was a jar and on top of it, coated with ash, was this one gold coin."

"There's your proof," Baba said.

Baldev looked bewildered as he turned to leave the gurdwara.

"Here, take some *prasad*," a man said to him. "A little bit will quell your hungers."

Baldev received it in his cupped hands and stumbled out, while Gareeb sat down at Baba's feet, feeling better than he had felt in a long time. A few strong young men volunteered to fix Gareeb's leaky roof and fetch firewood for him, while another offered him money to buy shoes for his children and a stove for the winter. A merchant offered bolts of cloth, a tailor promised to sew new clothes for his family, and Baba ordered five sacks of wheat flour and pulses to be delivered to his house on the bullock cart.

Looking at the audience, Mardana could tell that the story they had just witnessed had made an impression on them. How could it not? The event, together with the manner of its unfolding, had given them a glimpse into the mystical workings of the universe. Being in the presence of the Awakened One, the Master, the corporeal manifestation of the invisible and everywhere-present, breathing plasma of God, was magical. Baba was the horn that blew itself without any hands or lips, a note that echoed the *anahad shabad*, the illimitable, unheard primordial sound whose vibrations produced the visible world.

Compared to Baba Nanak, Mardana knew that he, even at the end of his life, hadn't even begun on the Path. He was Baba's shadow, and this thought, instead of making him feel inadequate, made his heart leap with joy. How grateful he was to have been allowed to be some small part of Baba!

When the singing and prayers were over, Mardana touched Baba's feet with an entirely new reverence. As he moved out of the gurdwara to walk home, Taru Poppat ran after him and threw himself at his feet.

"Bhai Mardana Jee, please, please tell me stories of Baba Nanak."

"I'll tell you," Aziza volunteered. "I know many."

"Yes, you'll tell me, too. But I want to hear from you, too, Mardana Jee. I will fetch and carry for you and do whatever you ask me to!"

Mardana lifted him up from where he had collapsed near his feet and said, "Bhai Buddha Jee, let's exchange stories. I will tell you what I know, and you will tell me what happens at the dera, for I am getting too old to come every day."

Bhai Buddha jumped up and down excitedly and said, "Yes, yes, I will tell you everything. It will give me another reason to stay with Baba Nanak all the time!"

Dear Readers,

It is time to leave Mardana here, walking home, the glow of Nanak upon him, always alive and undying in the pages of history, masterfully negotiating the crests and troughs of his life, nurturing the ember of love for the Supreme Being in his heart, fanning it with attention into a conflagration.

If the Beloved One so wills, we shall encounter him once more at the end of his journey; for this story, which skirts the far edges of what Baba calls *akath kathaa*, the Untellable Story, continues for another nine generations. For now, it is time to pause and end this particular tale with a beginning.

CHAPTER 24
Epilogue, Prologue

The sun, setting after a blazing display of color, has left behind a luminous sky awash with gentle clouds scattered in the heavens seemingly without plan, purpose, or symmetry, yet with a beauty so stunning as to captivate the eye of the beholder riding toward it, making him marvel at the miracle of light and sight, and the succeeding darkness in which seeds quicken, take root, and germinate. The stars appear to him like seeds of light scattered in the fields of an indigo firmament in which the barely visible, luminous arc of the new moon floats like a feather.

A stranger—a pilgrim, a priest with feathers in his turban, a dancer with bells on his ankles, a worshipper of fire, a spark seeking to obliterate itself in a flame, a singer with Nanak's songs reverberating in the chambers of his heart—rides on a white horse, a little girl sitting on the saddle before him, into the scene of our story.

In the cobbled streets of Kartarpur, he meets an old man with mud-stained clothes and a beard the color of the moon, accompanied by a young boy. He asks, "Could you please show me the way to Guru Nanak's house?"

The old man and young boy look at each other, smile, take the reins of the horse, and lead the stranger to his destination.

Bibliography

The following sources have been referenced for this publication:

Bal, Sarjit Singh. *Life of Guru Nanak.* 1969. Reprint, Chandigarh: Panjab University Press, 1984.

Goswamy, B.N. *Piety and Splendor: Sikh Heritage in Art.* New Delhi: National Museum, 2000.

Kohli, Surinder Singh. *Travels of Guru Nanak.* 2d ed. Chandigarh: Panjab University Press, 1978.

Macauliffe, Max Arthur. *The Sikh Religion: Its Gurus, Sacred Writings and Authors.* Vol I. Delhi:
     Low Price Publications, 2008. First published in 1909 by Oxford University Press.

Singh, Dr. Kirpal. *Janamsakhi Tradition: An Analytical Study.* Amritsar: Singh Brothers, 2004.

Singh, Harbans. *The Encyclopedia of Sikhism.* 3d ed. Patalia: Punjabi University, 2011.

The Electronic Sentence-by-Sentence English Translation and Transliteration of Sri Guru
     Granth Sahib. Translated by Kulbir Singh Thind and Singh Sahib Sinh Sant. Arizona:
     Hand Made Books, PDF.

CHAPTER I

Mardana's metamorphosis into a goat is a well-known legend. "The guru and Mardana went to Kamrup, a country whose women were famous for their skill in incantation and magic. It was governed by a queen called Nur Shah. She, with several of her females, went to the guru and tried to obtain influence over him. However, Nur Shah observed that her spells were of no avail." (Macauliffe, *The Sikh Religion: Its Gurus, Sacred Writings and Authors*, 73–78.)

The reference to Mardana becoming a goat is in *Travels of Guru Nanak*, page 42.

CHAPTER 2

"Guru Nanak felt that Mardana was in need of a better rebec. The rebec, a musical instrument made of wood and steel strings, was not easily available then. On enquiry, it became known that Bhai Phiranda, a native of village Bharoana towards the southwest of Sultanpur, possessed a rebec and that he might part with it if so requested. Guru Nanak asked Mardana to get some money from sister Nanaki and then meet Phiranda and bring the rebec. Mardana went to Bharoana. This village, these days, falls in the Beas basin where the Beini rivulet falls in the Beas. Now a Gurdwara stands there in the memory of Bhai Phiranda. The latter himself came to Sultanpur and gave his rebec to Nanak." (Singh, *Janamsakhi Tradition: An Analytical Study*, 78.)

The other goats are an invention of the author.

For the stories about Guru Nanak's birth and childhood anecdotes, see Macauliffe, *The Sikh Religion: Its Gurus, Sacred Writings and Authors*, 1; Singh, *Janamsakhi Tradition: An Analytical Study*, 55; Bal, *Life of Guru Nanak*, 15–18.

For mention of Daulatan, see Macauliffe, *The Sikh Religion: Its Gurus, Sacred Writings and Authors*, 1. That she was Mardana's aunt is an invention of the author. The goats and Fatima are an invention of the author.

CHAPTER 3

For the story about Mardana's encounter with cannibals, see page 144 of *Janamsakhi Tradition: An Analytical Study*: "One got hold of Mardana and got ready to kill him. The guru also reached there, and seeing his resplendent face, the cannibal bowed at the guru's feet. The guru got Mardana released."

CHAPTER 4

This chapter is based on an anecdote about a bundle: "The villagers came and offered Mardana large presents of money and clothes. These he tied up in bundles and took to the Guru. On seeing them the Guru laughed and . . . asked him to throw them away, an order which he at once obeyed." (Macauliffe, *The Sikh Religion: Its Gurus, Sacred Writings and Authors*, 45.)

CHAPTER 5

For references to the many incidents about Guru Nanak's youth, see the following: Macauliffe, *The Sikh Religion: Its Gurus, Sacred Writings and Authors*, 23, 30, 32–33, 37; Singh, *Janamsakhi Tradition: An Analytical Study*, 60–73; Bal, *Life of Guru Nanak*, 16–17, 35, 37, 41.

CHAPTER 6

See: Macauliffe, *The Sikh Religion: Its Gurus, Sacred Writings and Authors*, 34; Singh, *Janamsakhi Tradition: An Analytical Study*, 73; Bal, *Life of Guru Nanak*, 41.

CHAPTER 7

See: Macauliffe, *The Sikh Religion: Its Gurus: Sacred Writings and Authors*, 71; Bal, *Life of Guru Nanak*, 61.

CHAPTER 8

See: Macauliffe, *The Sikh Religion: Its Gurus, Sacred Writings and Authors*, 45; Singh, *Janamsakhi Tradition: An Analytical Study*, 81; Bal, *Life of Guru Nanak*, 82.

CHAPTER 9

For the story about the stone, Salis Rai, and Adhraka, see Kohli, *Travels of Guru Nanak*, 35–36; for references to Babar, the Saiyidpur massacre, and bhang, see Macauliffe, *The Sikh Religion: Its Gurus, Sacred Writings and Authors*, 114, 120–121.

CHAPTER 10

See: Kohli, *Travels of Guru Nanak*, 35–36.

CHAPTER 11

This story was inspired by a brush drawing on paper, *Guru Nanak and the Great Fish*, at The Government Museum and Art Gallery, Chandigarh, India. First encountered on page 29 of *Piety and Splendor, Sikh Heritage in Art* by B.N. Goswamy.

CHAPTER 12

An invention of the author.

CHAPTER 13

An invention of the author.

For reference to the story of the ants, see Macauliffe, *The Sikh Religion: Its Gurus, Sacred Writings and Authors*, 118.

CHAPTER 14

An invention of the author.

CHAPTER 15

An invention of the author.

CHAPTER 16

An invention of the author.

CHAPTER 17

An invention of the author.

CHAPTER 18

For the founding of Kartarpur, see Macauliffe, *The Sikh Religion: Its Gurus, Sacred Writings and Authors*, 131–133; Singh, *Janamsakhi Tradition: An Analytical Study*, 204–205; Bal, *Life of Guru Nanak*, 112–113.

CHAPTER 19

An invention of the author.

CHAPTER 20

See: Macauliffe, *The Sikh Religion: Its Gurus, Sacred Writings and Authors*, 182.

CHAPTER 21

An invention of the author.

CHAPTER 22

For reference to Taru Poppat, or Bhai Buddha (some say his original name was Bura), see Macauliffe, *The Sikh Religion: Its Gurus, Sacred Writings and Authors*, 133; Singh, *Janamsakhi Tradition: An Analytical Study*, 204–205; Kohli, *Travels of Guru Nanak*, 18; Bal, *Life of Guru Nanak*, 136–138.

The rest of the characters are inventions of the author.

CHAPTER 23

See: Macauliffe, *The Sikh Religion: Its Gurus, Sacred Writings and Authors*, 69.

CHAPTER 24

See: Bal, *Life of Guru Nanak*, 135.

Acknowledgments

First of all, thanks are due to Raoul Goff for his spiritual vision and for faithfully facilitating my voice on my third book with Mandala; Courtney Andersson for her patient, enthusiastic, sharp, and incisive editorial input; Erika Bradfield for her kind support; Vanessa López and the editorial and design team at Mandala for another excellent job; Nikky-Guninder Kaur Singh for her open-hearted, generous support; Tom Hoover for timely feedback, encouragement, and a fellow writer's enthusiasm; Navtej Sarna, Roopinder Singh, Pashaura Singh, Harpreet Singh, Surjit Patar, and Hans Raj Hans for their time and generous support; Bhai Baldeep Singh, master rabab builder and musician, for his encouragement at a time I needed it the most and for inviting me to Sultanpur Lodi for the first-ever reading from the manuscript; Poonam Khanna and Seema Gera of The Government Museum and Art Gallery, Chandigarh, India, for help with the images; Amrit Bolaria for her interest and excitement; Raman and Perry Khatri, my first audience, for reading the entire manuscript with enthusiasm; Nanaki Kaur, seventeen years old, "already at the pinnacle of wisdom" (in her own words) for reading the entire manuscript and giving me valuable feedback; Kulmeet Singh for giving me the key to Gurbani sources; and most of all, my husband, companion, friend, and fellow artist, Payson Stevens, for invaluable support in every aspect of my creativity, and for providing a stable, stimulating, and loving home life in which to pursue my projects.

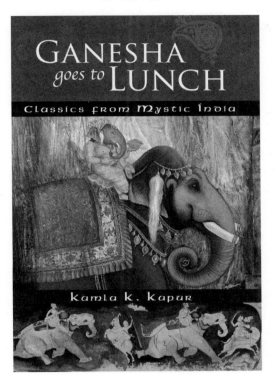

Ganesha Goes to Lunch

King Kubera was the greediest man in the world. Hated and feared by many, he schemed to win the love of the beautiful goddess Parvati . . . but learned an important lesson when he invited her elephant-headed son Ganesha over for lunch one day. So goes one of the many delightful tales in this decidedly grown-up book of traditional Indian stories, retold for the modern reader. Author Kamla Kapur is well known in her native India as a poet and playwright, and her connection to these age-old stories is the reverent yet individualistic one we might expect from someone whose introduction tells of her hometown, where naked, dreadlocked holy men speed about on motorbikes. To collect these stories, Kapur relied on ancient sacred texts, modern scholarship, and chance encounters with interesting people who just happened to know a really good story about the time that Vishnu sank into the ocean, was incarnated as a pig, and had a wonderful time. Like myths around the world, these are teaching stories that offer both a window into a fascinating culture that has endured for thousands of years, and a code for living that can be applied to the modern world.

$14.95 | Paperback | 978-1-60109-102-4

Rumi's Tales from the Silk Road

The 13th century Sufi poet Rumi traveled in a landscape divided between the Persian and Byzantine empires, and his works express the passions, fables, and faiths of both worlds. In this book, Rumi enthusiast Kamla Kapur reworks some of his writings into thirty tales of wit, wisdom, and faith. The basis for her stories is Reynold A. Nicholson's translation of Rumi's six-volume *Mathnawi*, an epic mystical poem of more than 25,000 verses. Kapur brings this dense, intimidating work into a far more readable form, putting her own spin on the stories, yet remaining true to Rumi's vision. In charming tales such as "The Witch of Kabul" and "Moses Learns a Lesson," she brings Rumi's verses to life as clever fables. *Rumi's Tales from the Silk Road* gives readers one of Persia's greatest literary treasures in an accessible form that enlightens as it entertains.

$21.95 | Hardcover | 978-1-60109-049-2 | Available anywhere books are sold.

MANDALA
PUBLISHING

www.mandalaeartheditions.com